BLOOD HINA

This Large Print Book carries th

Seal of Approval of N.A.V.H.

A MAS ARAI MYSTERY

BLOOD HINA

NAOMI HIRAHARA

KENNEBEC LARGE PRINT
A part of Gale, Cengage Learning

GALE
CENGAGE Learning™

Detroit • New York • San Francisco • New Haven, Conn • Waterville, Maine • London

GALE
CENGAGE Learning·

LIBRARY OF CONGRESS CATALOGING-IN-PUBLICATION DATA

Hirahara, Naomi, 1962–
    Blood Hina : a Mas Arai mystery / by Naomi Hirahara.
      p. cm. — (Kennebec Large Print superior collection)
    ISBN-13: 978-1-4104-2781-6
    ISBN-10: 1-4104-2781-1
    1. Japanese Americans—Fiction. 2. Large type books. I. Title.
    PS3608.I76B56 2010b
    813'.6—dc22   2010012728

Published in 2010 by arrangement with St. Martin's Press, LLC.

Printed in the United States of America
  1 2 3 4 5   14 13 12 11 10
ED190

For Sonia and Joyce

ACKNOWLEDGMENTS

My admiration for flower growers in the greater Los Angeles area reached new heights when I did research for a nonfiction book, *A Scent of Flowers: The History of the Southern California Flower Market, 1912–2004.* My memories of conversations with Ken Osaka, Jibo Satow, Art Ito, Larry Nomura, Mas Yoshida, and Frank Kuwahara still remain vivid. Rest in peace, guys.

In terms of *hina* dolls, I send my thanks to my relatives in Japan and my mother for passing down childhood gifts that served as my visual inspiration. Alan Scott Pate's beautiful tomes, *Ningyō: The Art of the Japanese Doll* and *Japanese Dolls: The Fascinating World of Ningyō,* are recommended reading for anyone interested in this topic. Other helpful resources are Michael Evans and Robert Wolf's *Kokeshi: Wooden Treasures of Japan,* Jill and David

Gribbin's *Japanese Antique Dolls,* and Sanae Tsuchida's *Tsuchida Sanae no Shiki no Tezukuri Ningyō.*

In order for me to understand the detail required to make these dolls, a visit to the home of doll-making instructor Soki (Kimiyo) Sakaniwa was invaluable. Thanks also to Emma J. Coleman, office administrator of St. Mary's Episcopal Church, who allowed me to experience again the church's extraordinary stained-glass windows. A walk with Evelyn Yoshimura in her Mid-City neighborhood made that area alive with detail.

The town of Hanley is fictionalized, but Imperial Valley, steeped in agricultural history, is very much real. The Pioneers Park gives a very comprehensive survey of the area. Tim Asamen, a native of Imperial Valley, kindly shared the story of collecting rocks in Niland, which was incorporated here.

There is a myriad of books on cocaine and its proliferation in North and South America. They include the video program *The True Story of Killing Pablo,* produced by Wild Eyes Productions for the History Channel; *Cocaine: Global Histories,* edited by Paul Gootenberg; *From Silver to Cocaine: Latin American Commodity Chains and the*

Building of the World Economy, 1500–2000, edited by Steven Topik, Carlos Marichal, and Zephyr Frank; Tim Madge's *White Mischief: A Cultural History of Cocaine;* and Nick Schou's *Kill the Messenger: How the CIA's Crack-Cocaine Controversy Destroyed Journalist Gary Webb.* Also of interest are two memoirs; Jeff Henderson's *Cooked: My Journey From the Streets to the Stove* and William Cope Moyers's *Broken: My Story of Addiction and Redemption.* Don Winslow (*The Power of the Dog*) and Deborah Ellis (*Sacred Leaf*) have also created powerful fictional accounts.

I have been personally inspired by the work of my girlfriend, Diane Ujiiye, and the Asian American Drug Abuse Program in the field of substance abuse prevention.

I feel so fortunate to live in Southern California, where the Little Tokyo branch of the Los Angeles Public Library and Kinokuniya Bookstore always seem to have research materials that I need.

The eagle eyes of Sonia Pabley caught plot mishaps — I'll always be indebted to you, Sonia! Editors Diana Szu, Marcia Markland, and assistant editor Kat Brzozowski at Thomas Dunne Books, copy editor Cynthia Merman, and agent Phyllis Wender have been incredibly supportive during the editorial process.

Appreciation goes to Leslie Klinger, the 2007–09 Mystery Writers of America/Southern California chapter president and good friend, who actually paid good money to be immortalized in a Mas Arai mystery. (At least the money went to a good cause, Les!)

And of course there are the usual suspects: Mom, Dad, Jimmy, Sara, and Wes. Thanks for being in my life. It's not always easy, but it is almost always fun.

Akari o tsukemasho bonbori ni
Ohana o agemasho momo no hana
Gonin bayashi no fue daiko
Kyowa tanoshii Hina Matsuri

Under the light of lanterns
Peach flowers are blossoming
Five musicians playing flutes, drums
Today is a joyful Hina Matsuri
— "Hina Matsuri Song," first stanza

CHAPTER ONE

"And do you, Sutama Hayakawa, take this man to be your husband?" the minister asked, the third time that night.

Mas Arai, his hands shaking and wet, wasn't going to miss his cue again. He pulled out the simple gold band from the pocket of his windbreaker and, pressing hard, as if he had captured a sand crab from a California beach, held it toward his best friend, Haruo Mukai. And then, before it could be successfully transferred to the groom, the ring slipped from his sweaty fingers and plopped into the fishpond below them.

"Ah, *oogoto!*" screamed an old Japanese woman holding a clipboard and standing on a concrete walkway on the other side of the pond. "I think that koi is going to swallow it."

Before Mas could take any kind of action, Haruo's grandchildren had jumped into the pond, followed immediately by the grand-children of Sutama, who was better known as Spoon. Fish tails of milky white and neon orange thrashed through the water in between soaked pant legs. Would Haruo's or Spoon's side of the family take the prize?

Spoon, Haruo's pear-shaped bride whose bulky sweater was no benefit to her ample *oshiri,* held on to the railing of the bamboo bridge, shell-shocked. Haruo, his skunk hair carefully arranged to cover the keloid scar on the left side of his face, tried to smile. "Howsu one more try, Mas?"

This wedding rehearsal was a disaster from the very start. Spoon showed up forty-five minutes late, saying her youngest daughter had taken her car without telling her, so she had to wait for another daughter to pick her up. All the grandchildren, meanwhile, had arrived, pulling at mondo grasses, terrorizing the koi, running through the bamboo, and hopping on the worn bridge. Mas could just imagine the reaction of his fellow gardeners who tended the Japanese garden in Los Angeles's Little Tokyo for close to nothing. The Gardeners' Federation was big on "volunteer" — Mas didn't believe in it because you usually ended up losing more than you put in. And for what? A pat on the back and maybe a photo in the federation's newsletter. Mas preferred his charity be less visible, if visible at all.

As the bridge shook from all the commotion below, the minister, dressed in slacks and blue sweater, desperately held on to a stack of three lacquer bowls that were part of the *san-san-kudo.* Three, three, nine — fortuitous numbers, eternal numbers. Both Haruo and Spoon had sipped from the empty bowls two times each during the rehearsal. Tomorrow the bowls would be filled with sake — Mas wouldn't mind imbibing some rice wine right now.

Why was Haruo, at seventy-one years of age, even thinking of getting remarried? Might as well just buy two cemetery plots right next to each other and put a bow tie on one headstone and a veil on the other.

The two of them had met at the flower market, and their romance had bloomed while Mas had been answering an exceedingly rare call for help from his daughter in New York City. Perhaps if Mas had stayed in L.A., Haruo and Spoon's relationship would have never ignited. Because if anyone could put a damper on love, it would definitely be Mas.

Spoon was all right, Mas guessed. She was pretty quiet for a Nisei woman, the second generation to be in America, and when she talked, she was *assari,* a plain speaker who didn't bother to smooth out rough edges like those straight from Japan tended to do. Mas remembered how his late wife Chizuko could shuffle and arrange Japanese words like a master magician so that the unsuspecting wouldn't even realize that they were being rebuffed or insulted. She would have thought Haruo's remarriage was *kurukuru-pa,* plain-out crazy, but if she had been here at the wedding rehearsal, a perpetual smile would have been plastered on her face.

Even the men at the Eaton Nursery last week seemed mystified at Haruo's upcoming nuptials. "Why don't he just go to Vegas?" asked Stinky Yoshimoto, examining the sharp teeth of one of the metal rakes for sale. Stinky was king of bad ideas and he was fortunate that most in their circle didn't bother to listen to him. "There he could sneak in a game of *pau gow* and poker between the ceremony and honeymoon."

Except that Haruo was a former gambler, a recovering one, as he liked to say. Gambling fever had ruined his first marriage and he sure wasn't going to let it grab hold of his second.

"So you some kind of big shot in the wedding, I hear," Wishbone Tanaka chimed in.

Wishbone, the former owner of his own lawn mower shop, was always concerned with status, even in the puddle of a world that they all inhabited. "Best man — *oshare, ne.*"

"Best man" did sound highfalutin. Mas had never been best at anything in his life, other than perhaps regrets. Haruo could have easily selected Tug Yamada — a medal-laden veteran who was trusty and dependable and would never do anything like lose the bride's wedding ring to a giant fish. Or even Wishbone, who limped around with a walker, its back metal legs protected by two neon green tennis balls, would perhaps have been a better choice.

But Mas and Haruo shared something that none of those men did — the Bomb. While the experience was written all over Haruo's scarred face, it remained hidden in Mas's heart and mind. The two men hadn't known each other in Hiroshima, but when they learned that they both had been in the city during World War Two, their connection was forever fused together. Haruo talked too much, but his overflowing words often greased Mas's disjointed emotions.

So when Haruo asked him to serve as his best man, Mas hemmed and hawed, but they both knew that Mas would eventually

17

give in. He always did.

Haruo now must have been regretting his choice, after Mas had presented him with the ring at the wrong time two times at the rehearsal and now it might be lost forever. The children were soaked and their parents, including two of Spoon's daughters, crossed their arms, their anger ricocheting from the hubbub onto Mas.

Haruo's grandson stood up in the knee-deep water. "I got it, I got it," he said, holding up a glint of gold like a prospector with a lucky find.

"Ah, *yokkata*," the old woman, the wedding coordinator, said in relief. She then studied the sky, weighed down by gray. "It's going to rain tomorrow," she predicted. "That means good luck." Mas hoped the wedding coordinator was wrong. Good luck, in Mas's experience, seemed to always be followed with bad.

From Little Tokyo, the three generations of Spoon's and Haruo's families — with Mas and a couple of others tagging along — headed deeper into the city toward downtown Los Angeles's industrial Four Corners, where the Garment District, Produce Market, Toy Town, and the Flower Market all collided. It was amazing that so much

18

down-and-dirty commerce happened downtown, merely blocks away from the svelte high-rises and fancy hotels. Some of the business — at least at the produce and flower markets — happened before the crack of dawn, when trucks and forklifts moved bunches of gladiolas and carnations, boxes of strawberries and tomatoes, in the transfer of goods that would continue onward to Des Moines, Iowa, or even foreign countries.

It was a secret world, where only nocturnal men and a few women like Spoon and her daughters dared to tread. At night, outside the aging and sometimes crumbling concrete buildings, the human residents of Skid Row, as well as rats and cockroaches, ruled the streets. Those fooled by superficial appearances might think that Four Corners L.A. was only for the impoverished. But scratch deeper and there was money to be had.

Some of these deals were forged inside nondescript diners that seemed to have been around from the beginning of time, or at least the beginning of Los Angeles. These diners had plain-Jane faces and sometimes bars on their windows, but insiders felt as drawn to their counters and tables as they did to their own mothers' kitchens.

If old-fashioned breakfasts, mounds of hotcakes, melting butter, and fat, swollen sausages were the king in this neighborhood, then chop suey, a mishmash of tastes from the Old West and Far East, had to be the queen. So it was no surprise to anyone that Haruo and Spoon's rehearsal dinner was held at one of the standard chop suey houses in the neighborhood. This particular one was even a favorite of a former manager of the city's baseball team.

Mas's own mouth was salivating as the oval plates of tomato beef, egg foo young, and crunchy chow mein were placed on the lazy susan on their table. He was sitting in between Haruo and Spoon's oldest daughter, a middle-aged woman who seemed destined to droop in the same places as her mother. The daughter, Debra, seemed distracted by her teenage sons horse playing at the next round table, so Mas thankfully could ladle his chicken soup to his mouth in peace. With the plastic plates of food arriving, the boys calmed down, allowing Debra to sink her teeth into her food and also Mas.

"So, Mr. Arai, are you still working?"

Mas removed a chicken bone that was caught in between his dentures. He hated that question. Seemed like once you hit seventy, everyone expected you to be good for nothing anymore. "Yah, gotta work." Even if it just meant a handful of customers.

Debra proceeded to ask question after question — Mas felt like he was the target of a firing squad, only here the shooter kept going even though he was dead. Did he have any children? *Yah.* Boy or girl? *Girl. Mari.* Did she live close to him? *Nah, New York.* East Coast? Why so far? It went on and on and on.

In desperation, Mas surveyed the table. He knew that Spoon had three daughters, the three D's. There was Debra next to him, Donna across the way, and Mas tried to remember the third D. He had run into a vanful of Spoon's girls and grandchildren at Haruo's Cracker Jack box–sized apartment in the Crenshaw District. The third daughter didn't look like the others, Mas remembered. She was skinny, but there was something else. Mas remembered that she was some kind of black sheep of the family.

Mas knew that the only way to stop Debra's prying was to aim some questions of his own. "Where's your sista?"

"Donna, she's right there." Debra gestured her fork toward the pear-shaped woman across from her.

"Nah, the otha one."

Debra's distaste for her youngest sister was apparent. "She couldn't make it."

She then bit down, even though it was apparent that nothing was in her mouth.

Mas's strategy worked, because the middle-aged woman promptly turned her attention to the person seated on her other side — Haruo's daughter, who was as sweet and gentle as her father.

Mas felt bad, but only for a minute as he scooped another helping of the fried rice drenched in soy sauce. He remained blissfully alone with the sound of the crunching of his food until someone began clanging his water glass with his fork. Others joined in and soon all the guests were focused on Haruo and Spoon.

"Kisu, kisu," he heard someone, most likely an old gardener who had drunk too many beers, chant from a corner.

Mas covered his face with his right hand. He had already witnessed his friend kiss his fiancée on the mouth three times at the rehearsal. Did he have to be sitting right next to him when he did it again?

Haruo noticed Mas's discomfort and began to laugh when he finally caught his breath after one especially long smooch.

"Mas, youzu just wait. Your turn's

comin'."

Mas knew what Haruo was getting at. Haruo had invited their professor friend, Genessee Howard, to the wedding tomorrow. Genessee was just a *tomodachi,* a friend. How could she be more? She was a professor at UCLA, after all. Why would any woman with a head on her shoulders want to be romantically involved with Mas? He was out of her league and Haruo was so blind with his own version of love that he couldn't see it.

Mas picked up an almond cookie from the lazy susan as Itchy Iwasaki, one of the heads of Lopez, Sing, and Iwasaki Mortuary in Lincoln Heights, approached their table. Mas wasn't quite sure why he was there — this event was for the living (well, at least barely), not the dead — but Mas remembered that Itchy was distantly related to Spoon through marriage.

"Good to see you at the track, Haruo." He tugged at one of his trademark enormous ears. "Haven't been there in years. No need to bet on-site with computers and everything."

"Oh, yah, good to see you, Itch." Haruo awkwardly tried to change the subject to the mortuary — "business good, must be with all these funerals" — but Mas's ears kept ringing. The track was off-limits to Haruo, at least according to his counselor in Little Tokyo. What was Haruo doing at the track, especially now that he was going to be a married man?

"I'm not feeling too well, Haruo," Spoon pronounced loudly, her fortune cookie, broken but not eaten, on a napkin in front of her.

Both daughters, Debra and Donna, looked across the table with concern and accusation.

"It's probably from the MSG."

"I told them no MSG."

"But you know there's always MSG."

As the two sisters argued, Mas's head started to pound. Leftovers had been scooped into take-out boxes and bagged. Only more small talk awaited. As the best man, Mas was obligated to hang around, but assisting the bride-to-be was as good an excuse as any to make his getaway. He turned to Haruo, who was holding Spoon's wrinkled hand. "I take her home," Mas said.

"You sure, Mas?"

"Yah. Get there faster if I go."

Haruo glanced over to the adjoining table of teenagers throwing chow mein noodles at each other and nodded his head. "Think you're right."

24

Spoon was obviously of the same mind because she nodded as Haruo whispered their plan in her ear.

The two daughters were not happy — each vied for the right to escort Spoon home until the old woman finally had enough. "Mas is taking me home. He is alone and has no one to worry about but himself and Haruo needs to pay the bill."

With that, the daughters finally complied. Mas could have taken Spoon's words the wrong way, but she had spoken the truth, no denying it. Mas was indeed very much alone.

They walked out of the room, past the counter where crooked framed photos of Dodger baseball stars were displayed on the wall. Mas grabbed two plastic-covered toothpicks and offered one to Spoon as they left the restaurant. She shook her head and Mas led the way toward his Ford truck parked on the far corner of the gravel parking lot. Since it had been stripped after being stolen some years ago, Mas had been busy improvising. In addition to the banana peel–colored car seat from a 1970 Chevy and a dashboard from another Ford truck, he had found a side mirror from a semi in the junkyard. With help from his friend Tug, Mas was able to weld and screw on the mirror on the driver's side. It was guaranteed that no other 1956 Ford could boast such an impressive mirror. While Mas was proud of the Frankenstein surgery on his vehicle, he sadly realized in the dim light of the chop suey parking lot that others might have a different opinion.

He took out a screwdriver, which he used to open the driver's side door, and then opened the passenger's door. He swept an old rag over the yellow seat until Spoon stopped him.

"Mas, I'm an old routewoman. Little dirt never hurt me." She smiled and plopped squarely into the seat. Mas then wondered if she really wasn't feeling well or maybe she just needed an excuse to get away from all the people. Routemen and routewomen were like gardeners; they spent much of their day alone, but instead of mowing lawns, they were driving to faraway places, delivering palms to Palm Springs and birds-of-paradise to Disneyland. From Haruo, Mas knew that Spoon's late husband had been not only a routeman but also had studied botany at Caltech. A genius and a self-made businessman — how could Haruo compete with such a memory?

"I guess being a best man isn't all that it's cracked up to be," Spoon said as they were on the road to the freeway.

Mas was surprised. How could Spoon read his mind?

"You're a loyal friend," Spoon said abruptly, causing Mas to almost steer the Ford across the yellow dividing line. "I'm glad Haruo has you."

Mas stole a glance at Spoon, all folded up in her white sweater like melting vanilla ice cream. There was something in her tone of voice that sounded sad, as if she thought Haruo would need him more than ever.

The rest of the drive was quiet, other than the squeaks and shakes, ailments of the aging Ford on the 60 Freeway. Friends told him to donate the truck to some nonprofit (the talk of "volunteer" again) and get a tax write-off of the Blue Book value of the vehicle — maybe five hundred dollars, if he was lucky. But the Ford, even in its distressed, makeshift state, was worth much, much more to Mas than five hundred dollars. In fact, Mas would not accept any other car — new or used, circa 1960 or more recent — in its place. Yes, Spoon was probably right. Mas was indeed loyal and the more broken-down you were, the more loyal Mas was.

City banners bragging MONTEBELLO with an image of a flower drooped from lights on the main boulevard. Mas faintly remembered the rows of greenhouses all over the city in the fifties, although now the only flowers that seemed readily available were the plastic kind Mas often saw in Mexican restaurants around town.

Spoon directed Mas to turn here and there. Finally they reached a plain wooden ranch-style house, probably built in the sixties when residential developments and smog had chased most of the flower farms and all of the fruit ranches from Montebello.

In most cases, Mas would have stopped just long enough for a passenger to jump out of the truck, but today was special. It was the night before Spoon was getting married, and Mas knew enough to walk her to the door.

"There's something I want you to have," Spoon said. "C'mon in while I look for it."

Mas wanted to go home, but he obeyed and followed her into her house. A skinny girl with long hair lying on her back on the couch looked up toward the open door. The missing daughter — freckles all over her face. *Sobakasu bijin,* they used to say in Japan. Buckwheat beauty. Although this girl's freckles looked more like buckshot that had taken beauty out of her years ago.

Still, there were remnants of something —
high cheekbones and a well-defined chin —
that resembled beauty for a moment in the
right light.

"My daughter Dee. I think that you might
have met her before." In response to the
introduction, the girl turned over on her
belly like a piece of bacon that was close to
being burned on one side.

Mas didn't resent the cold reception. Her
not talking to him meant he didn't have to
talk to her. But why hadn't she gone to the
rehearsal or dinner? She must have been
the one who had taken off with Spoon's car.
She looked at least forty — a little too old
to be pulling a high school stunt like that.

Haruo had mentioned something about
the girl being in some kind of trouble. She
was trying to get back on her feet and
Spoon and Haruo had both offered to take
her in. Mas's daughter Mari would never
think of moving in with him under any
circumstances. Well, she had a husband, a
giant blond *hakujin* gardener, and a young
son now. For a long period of time, they
barely talked, but now as Mari edged toward
middle age, no month would pass without
father and daughter speaking on the phone.
Sometimes their conversations were brief.
"Hi, Dad, how are you?" "*Orai.* Not dead

29

yet. Howareyou?" "Takeo's doing well in school." "Datsu good." "Well, talk to you later." *"Orai."*

Their simple conversations would seem superficial to most, but Mas felt the weight of Mari's phone calls — hearing her voice stoked embers of memory and feeling, which stayed warm for many weeks until she called again.

Mas stuffed his hands in his jeans pockets and circled the small but tidy room. There were photos on a long side table, quite a few of Spoon with her late husband, Ike. Mas hadn't ever met Ike, but he looked like a typical Nisei man, a dime a dozen. He had been thin with a thick crop of hair that seemed to progressively gray with each photo. He wore aviator glasses perched on a respectable nose, pretty high bridged for a Japanese.

Mas wondered if these photos would be removed once Haruo officially moved in after the honeymoon in Solvang, a Danish village up the coast full of hotels with windmills. Haruo would never insist on it. While most men would be threatened by images of past lovers or husbands, Haruo proudly accepted them like members of his extended family. "You knowsu, Ike was a big shot in flowers? People all ova, even in

Europe and Latin America, wanna talk to him."

"Ike supposed to go to camp in Arkansas, but gubernment sent him to Manzanar instead. Worked on a top secret farming project ova there during World War Two. *Hontō, yo,* no lie. Afta war, served ova in Japan."

"Ike met Nancy Reagan one time. Yah, at White House and everytin."

Finally Mas couldn't take it anymore. "Sounds like you gonna marry Ike, not Spoon."

"Can't help it. Nuttin' wrong in being proud of Spoon's first husband."

Never heard you brag about your own ex-wife, Yasuko, Mas thought to himself. But then Haruo had lost his wife and house to craps, not death, so that might not be a thing to dwell on.

Mas shifted his weight from one foot to the other as he waited for Spoon to reappear in the living room. The Buckwheat Beauty continued to ignore him, so he strayed to a fireplace where an elaborate display was concocted out of stacks of shoe boxes.

They were Girls' Day dolls. On the bottom level was a line of five musicians carrying drums and flutes. The second row, a line of three women dressed up in white and red

31

kimonos. At the top were the royal couple, the Odairi-*sama* and the Ohina-*sama*. In the Hiroshima countryside where Mas and his family grew up, they didn't have such elaborate displays, but he knew Chizuko's family had. In fact, when Mari was born, Chizuko's relatives attempted to round up a family Hina Matsuri display, but all had either been burned up in the Bomb or eaten by bugs and mildew. They said that they could send over a new one, but Chizuko told them not to bother. They were part of America now, and old traditions needed to die.

Obviously the Hayakawa family didn't feel the same way. Mas noticed that sometimes when multiple generations pushed the family tree farther and farther away from Japan, the new ones ran in the opposite direction to embrace the past.

As Mas slipped on his old Thrifty reading glasses that were in his pocket, he could more clearly see that the dolls on the bottom rungs were of the discount variety. The musicians were actually made of cheap mass-produced ceramic, probably circa Heisei period, 1989 to now. And with the benefit of twenty-twenty eyesight, Mas realized that the three maidens were actually plastic cartoon cats dressed in pink kimonos. Just *omocha,* nickel-and-dime toys.

The royal couple, the top dogs, though, were different. They had exquisite white faces — wisps of eyebrows on high foreheads, fine aquiline noses, puckered V mouths, and fine detailed eyes whose black pupils seemed to follow Mas's gaze. On their foreheads were two ash gray smudges, minithumbprints. Both figurines, dressed in colorful, multilayered kimonos of silk brocade, were seated on fat pillows, their arms outstretched in front of them. The man, his hair topped with a tall hat shaped like a gourd, was holding a paddle, while the woman was clasping a fan. Mas noticed that their wooden hands even had long distinguishable fingers.

Mas was about to poke one of the *hina* dolls when Dee stopped him.

"Ah-ah-ah," she said. "No touchy. Those two dolls on the top are old. My father brought them back after being in the army in Japan. I think from a place called Fukushima."

Mas grunted. He had known of other flower growers originally from the same area.

"Girls' Day's on Monday," Dee said.

"*So-ka,*" Mas acknowledged. The Girls' Day Festival, or Hina Matsuri, was on

33

March 3, three-three. What was it about that number? The only acknowledgment of Hina Matsuri in the Arai household came yearly from Mari's Japanese school in the form of *sakura mochi,* a confection of sticky pink rice kernels formed around a glob of red bean and then wrapped in the salted soft leaf of a cherry tree.

"I've been reading up on Japanese dolls." Dee tapped a thick book on the coffee table. It seemed to weigh a good ten pounds. Mas knew that a good steak cost about ten bucks per pound and wondered if that was the case with books. "You know that Girls' Day actually first had nothing to do with girls or daughters."

Eliciting no response from Mas didn't stop Dee from sharing her new knowledge. "It's all about sin and curses," she said, narrowing her eyes. Her voice took on a hushed, syrupy tone — Mas knew that she was enjoying herself.

"All the bad actions committed by a person would be transferred to these dolls. Not these fancy kinds, but paper ones. Then the people would crowd a boat full of these dolls and set them out on the seas."

And then? Mas waited.

"Sometimes they would even set them on fire. The dolls were scapegoats. You know, the things that people blamed unfairly. But then later on, the Wal-Marts of the Japanese samurai took over and made them into something for children, to protect the home and honor the emperor. Told families that their daughters would get married only if the *hina* dolls were brought out. Three-three on the lunar calendar. The time the peach blossoms should be blooming."

Momo trees had once been grown in Montebello. From a distance during the height of their season they looked like pink snow suspended in air. It made sense that a tradition like Girls' Day would be tied into growing plants. Almost everything Japanese — like surnames — had some connection to nature. Didn't matter that the *momo* trees in Montebello had been uprooted. Everything began in the dirt and ended there too.

"You're supposed to have a full court of fifteen, so we had to improvise," she said, referring to the toy cats and cheap substitutes. "But what really matters are the emperor and empress. Ours, you know, are haunted. My mother says they talk to her, especially the man — the emperor, right?"

Nanda? What nonsense was Spoon spouting? Maybe at her advanced age, her mind wasn't working quite right. That might explain her decision to marry Haruo.

"I have met you before." Dee sat up, pulling her skinny legs toward her body. "At Haruo's apartment, right?"

Mas nodded.

"You're the best man?"

Mas nodded again. *These Hayakawa girls sure liked to ask questions.*

"Don't you think that he's too old to be getting married again?"

Although he most definitely did, Mas shrugged his shoulders. "None of my bizness."

"I think it's your business. If you're the best man, you're the best friend, then. Or are you just bullshitting everyone?"

The girl was confusing Mas. And upsetting him as well. Never mind what Mas truly thought, what right did this *hoito,* beggar, have to judge her elders' actions and use profanity on top of that? She was the one who was taking advantage of her mother's weak nature and Haruo's good one to let her crash in her childhood home when she should have been on her own for the past twenty years. For her sake, in fact, Haruo was bucking common practice and not officially moving in until after the wedding ceremony.

It was then that Haruo's beat-up Honda rattled up the driveway.

"I'm going to bed," Dee announced suddenly. As she got up, Mas noticed how her jeans hung loose at her hips, revealing a pierced navel. She gestured toward the door before she left the room. "Tell him to lock the door when he leaves."

Mas didn't waste much more time in Montebello. There was obviously some kind of strain in the household. Mas wasn't sure if it was from the washed-up freckled-face beauty or maybe the stress of the wedding. But something wasn't quite right with Spoon, who had returned to the living room without whatever she was supposedly looking for.

She didn't seem too happy to hear her husband-to-be knocking on the door. "Haruo, you have your own keys, just let yourself in. This is going to be your house from now on. No *enryo*." What happened to all that kissing mess in the restaurant? It seemed that all that affection had evaporated once Spoon had returned home. If this was a sign of things to come, Mas wouldn't be seeing Haruo that much anymore.

Mas said his good-byes to the couple, eager to be released from so-called domestic felicity.

The rest of the evening was the usual.

Terebi, television, a Budweiser, and a swig of generic Pepto-Bismol to help his stomach recover from chop suey. Just like any other good thing, there was always a price to be paid.

Sleep came fast — first in his easy chair and then at two o'clock in the morning on his sheetless mattress. He rolled himself in a blanket made by Chizuko; sometimes he could imagine the touch of her calloused fingers moving the crochet needle back and forth.

The ringing of the phone awakened him. "Hallo," he spoke into the handset. His mouth felt pasty and he moistened his cracked lips with as much spit as he could muster.

"Mas." It was Haruo.

Sonafagun. Mas blinked hard, his hand reaching for the alarm clock. "Izu late?"

"Itsu not that," Haruo said. The reception was bad and Mas could barely hear his friend's voice above the static. Where the hell was Haruo calling from?

Haruo continued, "Wedding's cancel."

"Gonna rain?"

"No, Mas, itsu ova. No wedding no more."

CHAPTER TWO

Mas had seen Haruo in bad shape before. The worst was when he helped Haruo move into his one-bedroom apartment in the Crenshaw District after the divorce had taken away his house and his children. Haruo had let his hair grow even longer than usual so that it practically circled his neck like a scarf. He stopped shaving so that even the scarred side of his face, the left, started sprouting long, sparse, wiry whiskers that resembled those on a catfish. Mas, who usually didn't take much stock in appearances, had to admit even he was a bit revolted. If he had run into Haruo on a street corner, he would have immediately crossed to the other side.

When Haruo fell into depression, he didn't hole himself up in his apartment. No, he'd wander out to card clubs in Gardena, casinos in Hawaiian Gardens, underground poker games in San Gabriel — anything that would divert his attention from his insides. He'd place bet after bet on green felt tables until his pockets were empty, and then would make deals with Mama-*san* loan sharks out in the parking lot, mortgaging any last thing he owned at the risk of his life. Haruo would often even forget to eat. Actually, gambling would start to feed off of his body, taking anything good and productive and fueling it into chances, odds, and promises that never seemed to materialize.

It pained Mas to witness his friend transform into this frenzied and emaciated state, especially since Haruo's usual sunny optimism was the only thing able to pull Mas out of his own dark slumps. So Mas wasn't happy to be driving out to Crenshaw this morning, fearful of what he might find when he arrived at the chain-link fence around Haruo's rent-controlled duplex. Haruo had disconnected his telephone a couple of days ago in preparation for his new marital status and residential move, so he had been making his calls on a sticky pay phone outside a neighborhood liquor store. Trouble was Haruo kept running out of change to feed the phone. The only way Mas could continue their conversation without being cut off was in person.

Two bony ankles in zori slippers were visible underneath the Honda Civic in the driveway. Mas's heart leaped — surely Haruo hadn't done anything drastic — and he pulled desperately at one of the feet. Haruo was actually heavier than he looked and Mas didn't get very far. "Ah —" and then a hollow sound of something banging against the bottom of the car. A few moments later the legs squirmed out from below the car and Haruo, his clothing smeared with black oil, emerged.

"Mas, itsu you. Thought maybe youzu the neighbor kid." Haruo rubbed his oily hands on the front of the torn jumpsuit he was wearing over his jeans and T-shirt. He was having car problems, he explained, and was hoping an oil change would be the magic solution. He then told Mas to go into the duplex while he washed himself off with the garden hose.

The apartment was as bare as Mas had ever seen it, making it look much smaller than it really was. Only boxes, like giant building blocks, sat atop each other on the threadbare rug. A plain black suit, a clearance item from the now shuttered Joseph's Mens Wear in Little Tokyo, hung from a wire hanger from one of the grooves of the heater against the wall. The suit had been for funerals but was going to be baptized for a happier occasion today. In fact, the ceremony would have been happening in four hours from now, Mas noted, as he glanced at his Casio wrapped around his wrist with twine.

Haruo, who had shed his messy jumpsuit outside on the stairs, must have noticed Mas's sad examination of the empty apartment. "Yah, gotta find me new place now."

Mas frowned.

"Already tole landlord I'm gonna move out. If I wanna move back in, have to pay double."

Mas felt a streak of pain surge down into his toes. Sonafugun. Haruo's Social Security barely covered the cut-rate rent he had been paying for the last fifteen years.

Haruo shrugged his shoulders. "*Shikata-ganai,* huh?" Mas used to be a big proponent of *shikataganai,* it can't be helped. Wasn't that the official slogan of most Japanese out there, at least of Mas's generation? Got thrown in camp. *Shikataganai.* Someone break into my house in broad daylight and take all our jewelry. *Shikataganai.* Insurance not going to pay for wife's experimental cancer treatment. *Shikataganai.*

Lately, though, *shikataganai* was starting to lose its charm. *Shikataganai* made you swallow your anger when you should be beating your chest and yelling. *Shikataganai* made you sit still when you needed to move forward. *Shikataganai* made you think that you deserved bad things. And Haruo, of all people, deserved a lucky break. No amount of *shikataganai* would convince Mas otherwise.

They sat in the kitchen on top of boxes, sipping on room temperature Budweiser like morning orange juice. There was nothing else to drink, and Haruo, anyway, seemed eager to embrace the temporary buzz of beer. Mas waited to hear exactly why Spoon had canceled the wedding. By beer number three, Haruo's lips really loosened.

"You saw those *ningyō,* you knowsu, the two ole dolls, in Spoon's house."

"Yah, for Hina Matsuri."

Haruo nodded. "They just gotsu those dolls and now they're gone. Pah — gone."

"Whaddamean, gone? Just see them last night."

"Somebody take them. Right there in the house. No one break in."

"Gotta be dat girl." Mas tried to remember the daughter's name. "Ya know, the *sobakasu bijin.*"

"Who?" And then Haruo laughed. "Yah, she gotsu freckles, but I don't know if she a beauty. Datsu Spoon's youngest, Dee."

43

Mas wasn't going to be a *sukebe* — nasty old man — and argue the pluses and minuses of the physical attributes of a girl young enough to be their daughter.

"Dee the one who saysu I stole the dolls. Spoon saysu dat I need to lay low."

"Dō shite?" Why in the hell should he? "Itsu not like they gonna report to police."

The pupil in Haruo's fake eye began to float out of position.

"You meansu they goin' to?"

"Not Spoon's idea. Itsu dat girlu, Dee. They already called the police, but takes them awhile to get there."

Mas cursed silently. "Anyway, what would you want wiz those dolls?" Kid's stuff, weren't they?

Haruo's right eye blinked hard, while his fake one stayed eerily open. "Saysu I sell them. To gamble."

Mas took another swig of his beer, his tongue feeling the sharpness of the open aluminum tab.

"I quit. You knowsu. After I meet Spoon, I don't even have the feeling anymore."

Mas placed the half-empty can on the linoleum floor.

"Dis Dee no fan of yours, Haruo."

"Tell me sumptin I don't know, Mas. None of those girls like me too much. Can't

44

blame them — their papa was a big hero."

Again, platitudes about the dead husband. "How did dat guy die, anyhowsu?" Mas expected to hear the usual — cancer, heart attack, complications due to diabetes. But Haruo surprised him.

"Jiko."

"Accident? What kind?"

"Truck went off the road. Down there in Imperial Valley. In a small town called Hanley, 1980s sometime."

"Whatsu he doin' ova in Imperial Valley?" Imperial Valley was a former dust bowl next to the Salton Sea, a pitiful pool of salt water trapped inland near the Mexican border. Mas had worked there in the tomato fields for a truck farmer, just one stop of many throughout the Southwest before he got into gardening.

"Some kind of flower deal. Heezu with his flower market buddy, Jorg de Groot."

"Neva heard of no Jorg de Groot. What kind of name isu dat?"

"Orandajin. Papa was a Dutchman." Both Mas and Haruo were well aware of the Dutch contributions to horticulture in California. "You seen their old farm, I bet. Right there on a hill in Montebello. Birds-of-paradise."

Mas thought back and nodded his head.

45

Sure, he did remember, he told Haruo. He had a gardening customer in Montebello at one time, in fact. A wooden ranch-style house like Spoon's only larger on a sloping hill. One day, a dog took off with Mas's lunch and Mas chased him into a field of birds-of-paradise. These plants were young yet. The long bladelike leaves hit just below Mas's knees. The flowers did indeed resemble birds, cranes with crowns of bright orange and beaks of dirty purple. From their clumped nests of leaves, the birds-of-paradise seemed ready to chirp and cry for food.

"Well, dat used to be Jorg de Groot's place," Haruo exclaimed after Mas attempted to describe what he saw. "Son moved the whole operation down to Oceanside. Widow lives right across the street from Spoon now. Dat Jorg and Ike longtime friends, even before the war. When Ike was sent ova to camp in Manzanar, it was the de Groots who watch ova his family's place. They took good, good care."

Mas had heard stories of such *hakujin,* black and Mexican do-gooders. Ones who didn't seek to gain from the Japanese being kicked out of California during World War Two. Ones who paid property taxes for the Japanese while they were locked up. Some

46

even went all the way out to the makeshift prisons at racetracks, deserts, and swamplands to make sure their former neighbors were okay. Those weren't the run-of-the-mill type people, however. Mas didn't know if the shoe had been on the other foot, he would have done the same.

"Anyway, both of them die, right on the spot in dat accident ova in Imperial Valley."

Mas bit down on his dentures.

"Spoon's daughters still pretty young, in their twenties. Dee being the youngest was Daddy's little girl, you know? Took it hard."

Mas nodded.

"So I guess that's why those Hina Matsuri dolls were a big deal for her. Jorg's wife, Sonya, just find out about them. In an ole safe-deposit box. No claim them right away so government sold right underneath her nose."

Mas frowned. Why would the Hayakawa dolls be in this other man's safety-deposit box? Didn't make any sense.

Apparently the Hayakawas were surprised as well. Turned out that no one alive in Jorg's family knew about the safe-deposit box, which had been opened in a bank in San Diego. The box had been free of charge at first, but the bank had instituted an annual fee a few years ago. Jorg, being dead, wasn't able to make the payments, which meant all the contents went up for auction.

"Some doll people ova in San Diego buy the whole thing. But then Sonya find out and tellsu Spoon whatsu goin' on. Spoon go on the computa and buy the dolls back, but they cost her and cost her good."

"How much?"

"She don't tell me, but I knowsu itsu a lot. Don't know where she got the money. Sheezu flat broke — tole me dat she don't even wanna a weddin' ceremony. But I insist. She got married in camp, you knowsu. Second time around, I figure she deserve a white dress."

Mas's mouth was full of beer and he took his time swallowing. So that's why Haruo had gone to all this trouble with the ceremony. He wanted to give Spoon something that she wasn't able to have behind barbed wire. The thing was, Haruo also didn't have an extra dime to his name, but he claimed that his boss, Taxie, had given him an advance against his wages.

"How long you stay ova there last night, anyhow?" Mas asked.

"Ten. Spoon so tired, she fell asleep on the couch."

Mas then remembered what Dee had told him to remind Haruo. "You lock the door?"

Haruo pulled and twisted a long strand of gray hair and his fake eye meandered. "I dunno if I did. I plenty tired too, Mas. I came back here, went straight to bed, and then my landlord bangs on my door in the middle of the night. Emergency, he say. Gotta call Spoon."

Haruo's stingy landlord, however, didn't let him use his phone. Instead, Haruo had to walk two blocks underneath helicopter searchlights — a nightly occurrence in this neighborhood — to the liquor store's pay phone to make his call.

Haruo didn't say anything for a while, and Mas feared that his friend would break down right in front of him. But thankfully, although Haruo's good eye was unusually shiny, no tears were shed. The pupil in his fake eye had somehow floated into its proper place for a moment. In the right light with his head down, a stranger would not have noticed how truly ravaged Haruo's face was.

Mas wanted to leave, but he knew that it was too early. He cleared his throat. "Whatsu her girl's story?"

"Dee? Oh, sheezu been in some trouble. Spoon been up late at night worrying about her."

"What kinda trouble?"

Haruo rested his grizzly chin atop clasped hands. *"Mayaku."*

Drugs? "Like *hiropon?*"

"They gotsu a lot of drugs besides heroin, Mas."

Mas frowned. When did Haruo become an expert on drugs?

"Sheezu been hooked on cocaine. And new ones dat they stir up and cook in a house."

Sonafagun. That explained her sallow complexion and that pierced navel. Mas had known some drug addicts in his time. Boys and even some girls who wandered amid the rubble of Hiroshima a year after the Bomb, their wasted bodies shaking from the effects of drinking gasoline and shooting *hiropon.*

"Started right after high school. Got better and then went downhill after her divorce. Went through rehab. You know, rehab, Mas?"

Mas sneered and said yes, even though he wasn't sure. But from the context, he knew that this rehab had something to do with drying the girl out.

Haruo, a recent veteran of counseling, thought that people could change, be transformed. But Mas was more skeptical. Based on his postwar experiences, drug addicts couldn't be trusted. Sometimes an old dog was just that, an old dog. The tricks that it knew would just be repeated, the bad ones more than the good.

What Mas didn't understand was why Spoon was believing her drug-addled daughter rather than her future husband. If her faith in Haruo was so shallow, then good riddance. He even expressed that to Haruo in so many words, but his friend wasn't going to accept any talk of Spoon's shortcomings.

After close to an hour, Mas got up and crushed the beer cans against the floor with the heel of his work boot.

"Listen, Mas, got a favor to ask."

Mas threw the flattened cans in a corner and waited.

"Spoon's been callin' everyone, tellin' them don't bother comin' to the garden in Little Tokyo. I got a few more on my side I gotta tell — Wishbone and Stinky. Do you think you can handle?"

Wishbone and Stinky were two peas in a pod. You tell one, then you've told the other. Mas said that he'd pass the word to them and made his way to the door.

"I'm *orai*, Mas. No worry, no worry." Haruo was forcing a smile, but Mas noticed that the sides of his mouth were trembling.

How long would it be before he was in those card clubs again?

CHAPTER THREE

Mas had half a mind to drive straight home and sit there, playing solitaire on the kitchen table. But a *yakusoku* was just that, a promise. Mas didn't make it a habit to make promises, but when he did he always honored them. So he was off to carry out his mission as a messenger of bad tidings to Wishbone and Stinky.

As it was Saturday morning, Mas knew that he could find them at Eaton Nursery in Altadena. Wishbone used to have his own place, Tanaka's Lawnmower Shop, but the property was sold to a beauty shop, which lasted only a year. Now the whole building had been razed to make way for condominiums, rabbit hutches that seemed to multiply like mold all over the area.

Wishbone was always chasing money, and judging from his lack of it, the chase was ongoing. That explained why he always seemed to partner with the shadiest men who traveled through their world of lawn mower shops, nurseries, and even retirement homes.

His sidekick Stinky was now working part time at Eaton Nursery, an old-time business nestled below the foothills of the San Gabriel Mountains. Eaton Canyon was the closest thing to Yosemite, as far as Mas was concerned. The canyon cut through brown hills speckled with yucca plants, poison ivy, and tree poppies, its blooms like sunny-side-up eggs quivering in the breeze. Eaton Canyon felt the change of seasons more intensely than anywhere else in the valley. Wildfires eagerly lapped up the dried-up brush in the summer, while heavy rains, which descended about every other year, accumulated in the concrete wash and sometimes overflowed into the first floors of homes. It was a wild and sometimes unpredictable region, which mirrored the personality of the residents who had been there the longest. They were the type who actually thought Wishbone and even Stinky, who didn't get paid but still went into the nursery every day, were charming, believe it or not.

Wishbone was already out front with his walker, directing a worker to load some ficus plants into the truck. When he saw Mas, his pockmarked face cracked into a grin. "Thought you be in your monkey suit by now."

"Yah, well, datsu why I'm here." It was best to get right to the point. "No wedding. Cancel."

"So Spoon came to her senses, huh?"

Why would someone automatically think that Spoon and not Haruo had called it off? Mas groused privately. His duty done, he was prepared to leave but was stopped by Stinky.

"What happen?" Stinky's pants looked like they were hand-me-downs from a man twice his width. A worn-out belt cinched the pants high on his body, just below his chest.

"You owe me an Andrew Jackson, Stinky," Wishbone interrupted.

Stinky hiked up his pants even higher. "You say two days. I say a week."

"Wait a minute." Wishbone dug into his pocket and pulled out a small spiral notebook. "Dang it," he said, perusing its pages. "Kamiyama bet that it would never happen."

Mas's stomach sank. They were wagering on when the Haruo-Spoon union would fail? His disapproval must have been written on his face because the other two men

55

grew quiet.

"Listen. Don't get that way, Mas," said Wishbone. "A full-blown wedding? At our age? Even you knew that it was a joke, right, Mas?"

"No one can blame him from gettin' cold feet," added Stinky. "I thought he'd run after the ceremony, but it's better to do it before, anyways."

"Haruo didn't do no kind of runnin'," Mas said.

"So it was Spoon! We should have wagered on that too." Wishbone's face fell as he contemplated a missed betting opportunity.

"No, Spoon's house just gotsu some trouble. A *dorobō* got into the house and took some dolls." The minute Mas spilled the details, he regretted it.

"And they think Haruo did it!" Stinky exclaimed. "Is he gonna be locked up?"

Mas shuddered — he couldn't let his mind go there. Haruo in jail? He'd probably smile for his mug shot and thank the jailers before being eaten alive inside.

Wishbone, on the other hand, seemed more interested in the stolen merchandise. "Dolls? These collector items?"

"For Hina Matsuri. Girls' Day."

"Those dolls worth anything?"

Mas shook his head. "I dunno nuttin'.

Anyways, Haruo had nuttin' to do with it."

"You know what I hear? Haruo been going to the track, regular like."

"That guy has a sickness, no doubt about it. Surprised you're not able to keep him from self-destructing, Mas," said Wishbone.

Mas's fingers pulsed with anger for a moment. One thing that pushed his buttons was *sekinin,* responsibility. He did try to run from *sekinin,* but if it ever caught him in a corner, he never backed down. And for Wishbone, of all people, to insinuate that Mas wasn't being a good friend was more than he could stand. "Came because Haruo tole me to. Made a *yakusoku.* And now itsu done." Mas drew out his screwdriver from his pocket.

"Hang around, Mas. We'll play some cards at lunchtime, *orai?*" Stinky said, cocking his ear like a mutt in the pound.

"Nah, gotta go." No time for these good-for-nothings. Mas stuck the screwdriver a little too forcefully in the Ford's lock, so it took him a few minutes to jiggle it around until the door finally unlocked. He jumped into the seat and held on to the steering wheel so tight that his knuckles began to ache.

The more Mas thought about Wishbone, Stinky, and the gossip that would no doubt dominate the lunchtime card game, the madder he got. It was like the time Yasuko finally left Haruo after he hit rock bottom. No one at Tanaka's Lawn Mower Shop seemed surprised. It was one thing to let a man walk dangerously to the edge, quite another for people to be entertained by him falling down.

Would Spoon and her daughter really report Haruo to the police? Why should Haruo be framed this way? He hadn't stolen those dolls. And while Haruo maybe could be seduced to the poker table, he never was an out-and-out thief, *dorobō*. (Mas conveniently forgot that Haruo had stopped making payments to his *tanomoshi,* informal Japanese bank club, when his gambling problem was in full throttle.)

Anyway, if Haruo had stolen those dolls, whom would he have sold them to? Haruo didn't have contacts with wealthy collectors. Mas knew that people these days were selling all sorts of things on the computer, but the most high-tech item Haruo owned was maybe a solar-powered calculator that he had gotten free at a community health fair in Little Tokyo.

The whole thing stank, and Mas regretted that it began with Spoon. She seemed innocent and sweet, but maybe she was actually a confection that had gone bad. Was there any way that Mas could reach the Hayakawas before the police did and convince them not to say anything about Haruo? Maybe Haruo was ready to give up and say, *"Shikataganai,"* but Mas wasn't going to be so accommodating.

Mas headed directly to Montebello, which practically was a straight shot on San Gabriel Boulevard, past a closed bowling alley that Mas had occasionally frequented, past Hong Kong cafés, Vietnamese newspaper offices, and Chinese supermarkets.

Mas finally reached Spoon's street. The house was locked up tight, its eyes to the outside world closed and draped. No amount of rapping on the door or pressing the doorbell resulted in evidence of a human presence inside.

Did the *dorobō* just come through the unlocked front door? Mas wondered. Or was the thief able to pry open a window? Mas traced the outside of the window frames. The old peeling paint on the sills seemed to have been in the same sorry state for many years. Maybe a back door or other opening?

Mas didn't think twice about pushing open the gate to the backyard. After all, yards were his domain. And Spoon's was apparently the last stop for wounded plants, most likely rejects of her plant delivery business. There was a Japanese maple with burned-out leaves hanging on bare branches like dead spiders. Hydrangeas with strange yellowish leaves. Even a cactus with a middle so soft that it was practically collapsing into itself. There was no evidence that anyone was attempting to restore the health of these plants. The backyard was the last way station for reject plants — a plant shelter where neglected trees and bushes spent their last days.

Mas couldn't help pulling out a few dead branches and stems from plant containers as he walked to the house. After brushing the dirt on his fingers onto his jeans, he studied the back windows and jerked on the security gate door to see if it remained locked. Pretty tight, he thought. Not so easy for an amateur *dorobō* to break in and out.

A dog barked a few doors down, most likely sensing a stranger's presence in the neighborhood. *Yakamashii,* thought Mas. Too noisy, foolish dog. He continued to check around the air-conditioner unit connected to the living room wall when he heard behind him in the yard, "Hold it, police."

The words clanged in Mas's head, which

was feeling quite hollow right now. Then a sense of dread seeped from his head to his gut. No, this couldn't be happening. This was a bad dream.

"Put your hands in front of you, palms up."

Mas slowly began to turn, but then the woman's voice became more forceful and louder. "Hands in front, palms up."

Mas shot his arms in front of him as if he were one of those comic sleepwalkers in cartoons. He then angled his open palms so they faced the sky. He felt a gentle hand pat his sides, his pant pockets, and finally his legs. Mas was thankful that he had left his screwdriver in the unlocked trunk.

Another female voice, this time speaking a language other than English. Mas thought he recognized the tones and rhythms from the Chinese television programs he flipped through on his way to find his Japanese soap operas on Sunday evening.

"Can't speak Chinese," Mas interrupted. "I'm Japanese." Well, really he was American-born, but this was no time to split hairs.

Mas was allowed to finally face his captors. He was surprised. There were two uniformed policewomen, looking as young as teenagers. The first woman had a boyish haircut but an unmistakably feminine face, while the Chinese one had long hair that was clipped back in a ponytail. Why would their parents allow them to do such danger- ous work?

"My friend Haruo lives here," Mas ex- plained. "Well, gonna live here. Well, was gonna live here." The police officers frowned, trying to make sense of Mas's story. The Chinese policewoman asked to see Mas's ID, and he quickly located his driver's license.

"When you say Ha-RU-yo, are you talk- ing —" The officer with the short hair pulled out a small notebook from her back pocket. "— About Ha-RU-yo Mukai?"

It took a couple of minutes before Mas realized that the policewoman was referring to Haruo. Why would Haruo be known to the Montebello Police Department? It could be only one reason — he was a wanted man, and that realization weakened his knees. Both officers came to his aid before he fell, setting him down in one of Spoon's lawn chairs.

The two of them must have had a soft spot for old men, because they let Mas catch his breath before peppering him with questions.

The first one, of course, was: What he was doing there?

Waiting to talk to Spoon, or Sutama, as she was known to strangers.

The second one: Did he know about the burglary that had occurred there sometime within the past twelve hours?

Mas didn't know how to answer that one. They obviously were on a search to find Haruo, and Mas didn't want to give them any ammunition to shoot him down.

Sure enough, Haruo's name came up again. "We understand that he's moved out of his apartment and has no access to a telephone."

Mas swallowed.

"Have you been in touch with him today? We sure would like to talk to him."

"Oh, well —" Chizuko often said that Mas looked like a fool most of the time, and he hoped that attribute was in full force now.

"We understand that he works at the flower market, so we'll be contacting him there. But if you happen to see him—"

Before Mas could agree to anything that he might regret, a familiar figure appeared between a stubby palm tree and bug-infested Chinese plum tree.

"What's going on here?" Spoon asked. She apparently had noticed the police car out front. "What has happened?"

"Hello again, Mrs. Hayakawa," the short-

63

haired officer said. The three of them started to banter like old friends. "We received a call from someone in the neighborhood that there was an intruder on the premises. We found this man here in your backyard."

"He says that he knows you," said the Chinese policewoman, who Mas learned was Officer Chang.

"Yes," Spoon murmured. "He's a friend of the family."

I'm no friend of your family, Mas thought.

"He's fine," Spoon said. "I was actually expecting him this afternoon." She averted her eyes from Mas's, choosing instead to study her overgrown Saint Augustine grass.

The other officer, Gallegos, referred to her notes. "Mas Arai. This was the man who drove you home from the dinner last night. We heard that you were admiring the dolls."

Mas was stunned. The Buckwheat Beauty had sold him out. What was she implying? That he and Haruo had been working together?

"I don't care about no dollsu," Mas declared truthfully. "Datsu girlsu stuff, anyhowsu."

The two officers exchanged glances, a smile creeping on Chang's lips.

"Well, since we're here again," said Gallegos, "you were going to get us the contact information of where you purchased the dolls in San Diego."

"Oh, Hina House," Spoon replied, mispronouncing *hina* like hyi-nah, instead of hee-na. "I have their website and address in the house."

Was the Montebello Police Department's investigation going to spread to San Diego, at least a hundred and fifty miles away? These two officers seemed thorough and tenacious, which perhaps would not bode well for Haruo.

While Spoon was in the house to retrieve the information, Officer Gallegos reminded Chang, "We have to also verify how much the dolls are worth."

"A little less than four hundred — that's what she said this morning."

"Yeah, but I mean from the vendor directly."

Mas sat on the lawn chair pondering the amount of the purchase. Where did Spoon get four hundred dollars to buy something as nonessential as dolls? Haruo himself said that his future bride was hurting for money. Why would she go out and pay so much for two lousy dolls?

The radios connected to the officers' belts, which had been buzzing with static, now clearly broadcast a female voice reciting numbers and a street address.

Gallegos straightened her uniform. "We have to get going," she said to Mas. "Can you tell Mrs. Hayakawa to contact us with the information?"

Chang handed her business card to Mas. "And tell your friend Haruo to call us." Leaving the backyard through the side door, she added, "And stay out of people's yards, okay?"

Mas didn't say anything in reply. He had to be in people's yards; that was his livelihood. Who was the *bakatare* who had reported him as some kind of thief? They should have known with his gardening truck that he was legitimate.

Mas followed the two officers out to the front yard and watched them drive away in their black-and-white squad car. Meanwhile, a woman across the street scurried back into her house. Mas couldn't make out the details of her face, but there was no missing her twine-brown hair that had been spun into a bird's nest on top of her head.

Spoon came outside holding a piece of paper. "Where did they go?" she asked.

Mas didn't want to waste any time with explanations and, in fact, attempted to delay the inevitable. "They found Hina House

66

information," he lied, taking the paper from Spoon's hand. "Why youzu tell them about Haruo?"

"I didn't. I didn't even want to file a police report. But Dee insisted. She's so attached to those dolls, you see. They were her father's. I told her that Haruo had nothing to do with the theft, but she's been against him ever since she moved back home and started work at the flower market. She thinks he's going to hurt me, just like her ex-husband hurt her. She can't believe that Haruo's past problem with gambling is just that, in the past. You'd think she'd be more understanding about addiction problems —" Spoon stopped herself as if she might have revealed too much.

She then looked wistfully across the street at the house where the woman with the beehive hairdo had disappeared.

"Who live there?" Mas asked.

"Sonya de Groot."

"You think she the one who called the police?"

"She could have. I don't know. We don't speak to each other anymore. We used to be very, very close. They even moved to this street because I lived here. After our husbands died, we were like sisters, you know, with everything we've been through."

Spoon went on to explain that the de Groots had taken care of their route business and even visited them when the Hayakawas were in Manzanar.

"But then we got into this awful silly fight —"

Mas waited.

"Over those dolls."

Sonya had been the one who told Spoon that the dolls had been sold at an auction in the first place.

"So I contacted the buyers — they were actually doll dealers in San Diego and the dolls were on their website. With the business, I can get around on the computer and started bidding on the dolls. I didn't know Sonya would be interested. I mean, they were Ike's, right? Yes, they were in Jorg's safe-deposit box, but she didn't know that they even existed before.

"She insisted that she buy them back from me, that her son absolutely wanted them back. I told her no, that I wanted to keep them for Dee. Dee was always so taken by them, even when she was little."

The whole thing was curious. Here was a do-gooder, who had stuck her neck out for a friend during a war, and who now was ready to sever ties over a doll.

"She hasn't spoken to me for a couple of

weeks, and for what? I miss her," said Spoon, her eyes watering.

Spoon wasn't the crying kind, so Mas knew that the widow was genuinely out of sorts with the loss of this friendship. But shouldn't Spoon be crying over her broken engagement instead?

Witnessing Spoon's misplaced sorrow over the loss of her friendship with her neighbor stirred up Mas's anger. How about some tears for Haruo?

Spoon must have sensed Mas's feelings because she seemed to cave in a couple of clothing sizes. "Have you seen Haruo? How's he doing?"

"No good," Mas said. He didn't bother to mention that Haruo had been found doing something as mundane as changing his car oil. "Gonna have to find a new place to live, you know."

"Maybe he could room with you for a while?"

Mas scowled, feeling any last bit of respect for Spoon evaporate. "He neva have dis problem in first place. He *orai* on his own before."

Pink splotches erupted on Spoon's usually pale face. "I wasn't the one who pushed to get married, Mas. It was all Haruo's idea."

"If you not ready, you shoulda tell him."

"I tried." Spoon's eyes were getting watery, so Mas knew that he needed to back down. "I told him that happily ever after doesn't happen for old fogies like us."

CHAPTER FOUR

When Mas and Chizuko's only daughter Mari became a teenager, she temporarily transformed into an *ohina-sama,* a pimple-faced princess who suddenly was above washing the dishes and taking out the trash unless Chizuko's nagging hit a high enough crescendo. At the time Mas wondered if he had been at fault. After all, during Mari's early childhood, Mas often went through his customers' trash, looking for discarded picture books or toys that featured a *hina,* an empress or princess, or any woman wearing a crown. Had he inadvertently sealed her fate by giving her one too many used Cinderella stories? Luckily, the *ohina-sama* phase turned out to be short-lived, but perhaps not short enough for Chizuko.

Now Mas again was searching for a *hina,* or at least two dolls of royalty. They weren't in a metal trash bin but in San Diego.

Turns out Hina House wasn't in the

ramshackle part of San Diego that Mas was used to. A navy town, San Diego's downtown had once been full of sailors wandering through dives and dirty streets, their hands wrapped around necks of beer bottles or women. Now the Gaslamp Quarter was lined with fancy restaurants and stores that would make the Las Vegas Strip blush. Even the area around SeaWorld seemed to have had a face-lift. Mas passed an airport (who knew San Diego would have such a high-tone one?) and then he hit a pretty hilly area right next to the water. It reminded Mas of a cleaner version of San Francisco or even Nagasaki (even though he hadn't been back there in fifty years). The sky was a brilliant blue — not the kind that made you take a few steps back in wonderment but so piercingly clear that it almost hurt your eyes.

This part of San Diego — Point Loma — resembled scenes on postcards Mas had received from time to time from his customers on vacation in France or Spain. In fact, the house on the hill had stucco walls, curved archways, and red Spanish tile, just like the European ones.

Outside in the yard were succulents of every type: ocotillo — little scarves of red poking out of its giant pipe cleaner spindles; jumper catci glowing like radioactive teddy bears; and plenty of medicinal aloe, its healing balm dripping from torn rubbery leaves. In the middle of the desert garden was a wooden doll attached to a wooden stake and the sign, HINA HOUSE.

Mas parked the truck on a slope, pulling at what remained of his emergency brake. Why was he here? He had pondered that as he drove on the 5, past the immaculate sheen of Orange County, the impressive shell of Angel Stadium, and sand-colored mini-malls scattered along the freeway. Only when Mas could see the water when he reached San Diego County did he feel more at home. The familiar dome of the nuclear power plant and the yellow sign warning of immigrant families who might be running across the highway suggested danger and desperation, two feelings that Mas could easily relate to. There was just something about Spoon's dolls. Perhaps it was how their pupils followed his, or maybe the care that their creator had taken to make them as beautiful and refined as possible, not necessarily for monetary gain but just for art and craft. Were they really that valuable? Enough for two old buddy-buddy women to split their friendship over them? Enough for someone to break into a house and take them? A piece of the puzzle was missing, and to help clear Haruo, Mas had to drive two and a half hours south to find it.

As Mas knocked on the large double doors of Hina House, he wondered what would be on the other side. This was a residential area, no sign of gift shops or anything below the radar. No one answered, so he resorted to the doorbell. He could hear the muffled tune of the Japanese folk song "Sakura," the sad ode to the fallen cherry blossoms, which always seemed to remind Mas of a funeral dirge.

The door opened, revealing a thin, skeletal man with a frayed wisp of a light-brown mustache. "Hello." He spoke slowly as if he were savoring each syllable of his words.

"Hallo."

"Can I help you with something?"

"*Ningyō.*" Mas must have uttered the magic word, because the skeleton man broke out in a smile and held open the door.

"Well, if you are looking for dolls, you've come to the right house."

Mas walked into an uncovered patio with a large pool. Floating in the water were blow-up dolls, Japanese cartoon ones with huge eyes reflecting stars and circles. Mas was always mystified by the size of their eyes, since Westerners always seemed to make mention of how small Asian eyes were.

Mas glanced back at the closed double doors. Perhaps he had made a mistake. What right-thinking man would have a pool filled with blow-up dolls?

The man waited for Mas beside another set of doors, these leading to the house. They were large sliding glass doors, tinted black. Why deface windows like that? wondered Mas. Obviously the man didn't want the San Diego sun to damage the contents of his house.

The man slid the door open and gestured for Mas to enter first. Mas hesitated for a moment. But then, hadn't he been the one to come knocking at the door of Hina House? Whether he liked it or not, Mas would have to see this through.

Stepping over the metal grooves of the door frame, Mas blinked hard — *pachipachi* — as his eyes adjusted to the darkness of the room. Most likely designed to be a living room, it was long and cavernous with a relatively low ceiling. Mini-spotlights arranged in different directions showcased — what else? — dolls. A small forest of wooden *kokeshi* dolls, armless and legless, was gathered together on a low platform.

Cascading down a red-carpeted six-tiered stand was an elaborate set of *hina* dolls. As was tradition for the Hina Matsuri, the bottom row had the minitrays of food and *tansu,* lacquer drawers, then a row of rickshaws followed by a row of male big shots. Above the dignitaries were five musicians, each carrying a different instrument. And above them, three ladies-in-waiting, each wearing a snow-white kimono.

At the top were the *dairi-sama* and the *hina-sama.* These dolls looked older and more ominous than Spoon's. Their faces were the same plaster white color, but this couple was outfitted with gold brocade kimonos that sparkled underneath the spotlight.

Mas felt his head spin, as if the walls and ceilings were closing in on him. He wasn't much of a fan of dolls; in fact, many of them frightened him. At Disneyland, for example, he disliked most of the rides, but the worst was the one called It's a Small World, in which you rode on a boat that took you through different countries featuring the same plastic dolls, altered only in skin color and costume. These dolls were attached to wooden sets and they moved mechanically, their eyes choreographed to blink simultaneously. The dolls also moved their mouths to the same tune sung in different languages, an infinite loop of cheeriness. It was enough for Mas to consider jumping ship into the knee-high water. But of course it was Mari's favorite ride, requiring him to accompany her over and over again.

"Is there something specific that I can help you with?"

"No, just lookin'." Mas attempted to stare down the emperor and empress on display. The dolls won.

"They're fascinating, aren't they?" the man interjected. That was one way to put it. "*Hina.* Short for small and lovely. Those are from the Edo period, the mid-seventeenth century."

The man gave the dolls a lover's look. "Americans often mistake dolls for toys. But these are items of royalty — kings gave them to one another. It eventually trickled down to the masses, as these things often do."

Hina House's proprietor then pointed to a series of larger warrior dolls wearing helmets and carrying arrows on their backs. "Those are the ones for Boys' Day, but they just didn't catch on like the ones for Girls' Day."

Mas nodded. He seemed to remember that at one time his own family in Hiroshima had a replica of a samurai helmet on display. And then every fifth of May, five moth-eaten carp banners were flown outside their house — that is, until World War Two officially started and killed all traditions.

The man bent down to pick up one of the wooden *kokeshi* dolls with a gloved hand. It was one of those typical types with a ball head and a long cylindrical body. The doll had eyes and a dot for a mouth and an ink wisp of a nose. Her costume consisted of colorful stripes. "Even this simple *kokeshi* can have layers of meaning. No one is sure of where the name *kokeshi* came from, but it might refer to the Japanese words for 'dead child' or maybe 'extinguished child.' "

Mas moistened his lips. Even though it was warm outside, it seemed as though a constant breeze was tickling his neck.

"Some maintain that the *kokeshi* represents the child killed in poverty-stricken households. But, of course, the *kokeshi* could be just what it is, a souvenir from a vacation at sulfur hot springs in the southern part of Japan."

Talk of killing children began to make Mas uncomfortable and he moved to the other side of the room, where an almost three-foot-tall kimono-clad doll was in a glass box. With a large spotlight focused on her, she was apparently the Shirley Temple of Hina House, without the golden curls and smile.

The Hina House man had followed Mas

to this side of the showroom. "That's our star. Our Friendship Doll. Miss Tsuneo." Noting Mas's blank look, he continued. "You've never heard of the Friendship Dolls? America sent about twelve thousand blue-eyed dolls over to Japan, while dozens of these magnificent Japanese ones were sent over to the U.S. in an exchange with Japan in the 1920s. Actually that's how I first got into this business. I was only a baby at the time, but my mother took a photo of me next to the Friendship Doll at the museum in Raleigh, North Carolina. Miss Kagawa was the only one on public display in the United States during World War Two. Most of the other dolls had been destroyed by their owners by that time."

The lifelike doll seemed to have real hair, Mas noticed. "Look like she breathin'."

"Yes, isn't she amazing?" The Hina House man seemed to dote on the doll and even began to sing a traditional lullaby to it: *"Nen nen korori yo, okorori yo."* Go to sleep, go to sleep.

As Miss Tsuneo's glass eyes showed no signs of closing, Mas felt the hairs on his arm rise. *Your doll is not alive!* Mas wanted to yell.

The man studied the top of the doll's head and tsked. "There's some dust in her hair.

Noriko," he called out.

Mas was growing more fascinated by and also repelled at the man's devotion to the doll.

A side door opened, revealing an Asian woman.

"Noriko, Tsuneo-*chan* needs some *sōji.*" The man remembered Mas and extended his arm toward him. "Oh, forgive my rudeness. This is my wife."

She herself resembled a *kokeshi* doll, with a small to nonexistent mouth and arms that stayed close to her narrow frame. Her mushroom-cap hair was a shiny sheet of blue-black. Even though Mas had been born in California, he obviously wore some of the years that he had spent in Japan, because the mushroom woman bowed deeply toward him. *"Hajimemashite,"* she formally greeted him.

"Hallo," Mas said in reply.

"I didn't get your name —" the husband said.

Because I didn't give it, thought Mas. But he offered, "Mas Arai."

The husband bowed and presented a business card with both hands. HINA HOUSE, it stated. *Les Klinger.*

Mas awkwardly accepted the card and then tugged at his wallet. He had an old

80

business card somewhere in an ignored flap. MASAO ARAI. ORIENTAL GARDENING, and his phone number and home address. The card was so old that it had the old Los Angeles telephone exchange for the Altadena-Pasadena area, Sycamore for the prefix 79.

The edges were so worn down that the card looked more oval than rectangular. It was all that Mas had, so it would have to do.

As Noriko excused herself to get some cleaning products, Klinger studied the card for a while, making Mas nervous. "Gardener. A venerated profession. It's always an honor to meet a gardener."

Mas wasn't sure what "venerated" meant, but he did understand "honor." Compliments didn't come his way very often, so he accepted the few that did, even when he didn't quite comprehend them.

"Altadena is in Los Angeles, *ne?*"

"Near Pasadena."

"You've come a long way. Surely your coming here is no accident."

Mas regretted sharing his business card. Now this Les Klinger had his personal information. There was no alternative but to tell the truth.

Mas cleared his throat. At least this man

obviously knew some Japanese. "I lookin' into a *ningyō,* one bought by Spoon Hayakawa."

Klinger frowned. "Spoon Hayakawa?"

Mas fished for her real given name. "Sutama."

"Hayakawa Sutama-*san,* of course." The Montebello Police Department had apparently not yet contacted Klinger, because he seemed unaware of anything negative befalling the dolls. "She had that splendid *Odairi-sama* and *Ohina-sama.* A wonderful representation of the early Meiji period. Excellent condition. We have a few others from the same time period." Klinger moved toward his computer, but Mas stopped him and explained that he wasn't interested in any others. "Just dat one."

"That's a very popular *ningyō.*" Klinger spoke carefully. Noriko had returned to the showroom with a key to open Miss Tsuneo's glass prison. She was using a miniature duster made out of what looked like silk cloth to brush the doll's hair. "May I ask what this doll has to do with you?"

"Spoon's my friend's wife." Mas stretched the truth to earn some goodwill. "Somebody robbed it. Spoon don't have it no more."

Klinger's face, which was already the hue of a manila folder, became even more ashen.

82

The smile on his face seemed to slip a few degrees south. He recovered quickly, but not quickly enough for Mas not to notice. "Well, I'm sorry to hear that. I must emphasize that Hina House is not responsible for anything that happens to our dolls after they are sold."

Mas had heard that line from storekeepers before. "How you know about it, anyway?"

"A state unclaimed property administrator contacted us. We're the foremost experts of *ningyō* in the state, maybe in the whole nation." Mas could hear the pride in Klinger's voice. "The doll set had been left in a safety-deposit box that had been abandoned. Banks are supposed to be more diligent in finding heirs of safe-deposit box owners, but most of those unclaimed are usually auctioned.

"We were just happy that Mrs. Hayakawa's dolls were returned to her, but to now find out that they were stolen is regrettable indeed. Please tell her that we certainly hope that the dolls will be recovered soon. I trust that she insured them, as we advised."

"Insurance?" Mas had never heard of people bothering to insure dolls.

"Yes, the one I advised can deal with a three-thousand-dollar purchase." *San-sen*

83

doru? Three grand? Mas thought that he had misheard Klinger.

"I know, terribly overpriced, I told both of them."

Mas couldn't believe that anything made out of straw, wood, rice paste, and shiny fabric could command such a high price. Even Klinger had apparently been surprised.

"I know, I know. But don't accuse me of taking advantage. There were two of them who wanted the dolls, so it was a matter of who wanted them more."

"Not just Spoon?"

"Oh, no, it went to auction. Didn't Mrs. Hayakawa tell you? She and another person bid on it over our website. I was going to cap it at about a thousand, but they both insisted that I allow them to go higher. Finally, I just put out a ridiculous sum — three thousand. It would either be the one who won the auction or paid that 'get-it-now' price. Mrs. Hayakawa was the one who beat Urashima Taro to the punch."

Urashima Taro? The Japanese version of Rip Van Winkle, the man who went to the Turtle World and partied for decades, only to return to his hometown a stranger. Mas at times felt like Urashima Taro in his home state, California, and that was without stepping one foot outside of it.

"Urashima Taro was his or, maybe, her computer name," said Les. "Since Mrs. Hayakawa won the auction, I have no idea who the loser is."

After leaving the dark showroom of Hina House, Mas found the sun a bit of a shock. In fact, the whole conversation with Les Klinger unsettled him. Spoon had told him, and even the police, that the display had cost four hundred dollars. Why lie? And the sum. How in the world could Spoon have come up with that money? Mas was so distracted that he almost rear-ended the car in front of him. The traffic snaked up a green hill that seemed to be eaten away by new housing developments.

What kind of trouble was Haruo in? It was one thing to be accused of stealing something worth four hundred dollars, but three thousand? If found guilty, Haruo could be locked up for a very long time.

Why had Haruo gotten involved with Spoon? No one told him to get serious with a woman at his age. The more Mas thought about it, the madder he got. Haruo had placed himself into this mess, so why did Mas feel like he had to get him out?

Haruo just needed to go away for a while,

Mas told himself. Take a vacation. Everything would probably blow over — the Montebello police probably had more serious crimes to worry about than two stolen dolls. Mas would just tell Haruo to keep his distance from Spoon as much as possible. Even though she seemed pleasant enough, Spoon was starting to smell *kusai* and Mas didn't want that stink to further ruin his friend's life.

After coming to his solution, Mas instantly felt much better. He even stuck his elbow out the open window and felt the wind blow on his cheeks and earlobes. He'd soon be home, enjoying a bowl of ten-minute boiled Sapporo ramen noodles. Just thinking about that salt on his lips and tongue made him salivate.

He turned on McNally Street and immediately noticed an old Honda, the red color faded and its doors battered with decades of dings, parked in front of his house. And a familiar figure seated on his porch beside two duffel bags and a suitcase. If Mas hadn't been spotted by his visitor, he would have done a U-turn and pressed down on the gas. But it was too late.

"You need to leave L.A.," Mas insisted to Haruo. "At least for a little while."

86

"Where I gonna go? Gotta work. *Shigoto* hard to come by these days."

Haruo was right. He was lucky to receive even his meager wages from the flower market. The demand for a seventysomething man with only one good eye was limited indeed.

"Nowhere else for me to go, Mas," Haruo repeated, now talking about living at Mas's house.

How about your own grown daughter and son? Mas said to himself. Haruo must have read Mas's face, and he added, "Don't want to be a *meiwaku* to Clement and Kiyomi."

And you want to be a burden to me? Mas silently answered back. But he did understand where Haruo was coming from. Haruo had just started to rebuild relations with his daughter, whereas Clement, a mama's boy, was less forgiving.

"I figured that you have all dis space just for you."

"*Orai, orai.* You stay, but only two weeks, *yo.*" Mas tried not to think about if Haruo overstayed that time period. That would be tomorrow's problem, not today's.

"Where you been, anyway? Been waiting here for two hour," Haruo asked him straight-out, and Mas at first didn't know what to say. Without knowing what was

87

really going on with the dolls and Spoon, it served no purpose to get Haruo all tied up in knots.

"Just had *yōji.*"

"Bizness? When you do have bizness, Mas?"

"I still have thingsu to do," Mas said a little too harshly. He was always sensitive to any insinuation that he might have a lot of time on his hands now that he was semi-retired.

"Well, another thing . . ." Mas waited. "My car's still not workin' too good."

"Saw it out on the street."

"Yeah, well, I had it towed ova here."

Chikushō, Mas cursed under his breath. The sheriffs ticketed for overnight parking, so the pitiful heap needed to be moved into the driveway. With Haruo in the driver's seat steering, Mas pushed from behind. The car had barely moved a few inches when some neighbor children joined in to help. When it came to broken-down cars in this neighborhood, it didn't matter if you were on your way to rob a bank or keep a date with a mistress. Everyone got a push, because that's the least each person deserved in this life.

They eased the car in the driveway and the children disappeared as quickly as they had appeared. Mas forlornly looked first at his Datsun elevated on cement blocks and then at the Honda. He now had two dead cars sitting at his house.

Dinner was next on the agenda. There was only one ramen package in the cupboard. So the noodles went to Haruo, while Mas was left with heels of old bread and some peanut butter. As the peanut butter stuck to the roof of his dentures, Mas could have cried right then and there at the kitchen table.

Haruo was smart enough to stay quiet for most of the evening. He washed his ramen bowl and even scrubbed the stained counter grout with an old Brillo pad and some cleanser.

Mas wanted to tell Haruo not to bother, but then they both believed in earning your keep. If this was Haruo's method of payment, Mas needed to accept it. "What time you gotsu to be at the flower market tomorrow morning?" Mas finally asked.

"I can take bus."

"I drive youzu," Mas said.

Haruo began to protest but then apparently thought better of it. "Gotsu be there by four."

Four it was.

"One thing, if you gonna hang around the

flower market, police gonna be callin' for you. Maybe betta if you go to them first." Mas removed Officer Chang's business card from his wallet and gave it to Haruo.

Just the mention of the police made Haruo's scar bulge out. "Izu don't wanna to talk to them. Don't they have to arrest me to make me talk?"

Mas sighed. It probably wouldn't be a bad idea for Haruo to avoid the police, at least for a couple of days. When Haruo was nervous, there was no telling what he'd say.

Pulling a cold Budweiser from the refrigerator, Mas escaped to his bedroom, where he read the Japanese newspaper he got in the mail. When he returned to the living room an hour later, Haruo was already passed out on the couch. Pulling a blanket crocheted by Chizuko over his friend's pitiful body, Mas couldn't see the knotted keloid scar. With his face pressed against the pillow in the dark light, Haruo looked normal, like any old man worn out from the day or his whole life.

CHAPTER FIVE

Mas didn't sleep well, which was always the case when he knew he had to wake up early. Rather than risk oversleeping, *asanebo,* he preferred to take the route of hardly sleeping at all. As a result, his eyes burned as he concentrated on the dips and turns of the Pasadena Freeway, the oldest operating highway in the nation. The freeway was full of deadman's curves — bashed guardrails and skid warnings of what lay ahead. Mas was ready to go when his time was up, but he was committed to leave the world alone — no plans to have anyone else's blood on his hands, especially a friend like Haruo's.

Haruo was currently chattering nonstop, wired from three cups of instant coffee. Usually such *urusai* talk so early in the morning got Mas in a particularly bad mood, but Haruo didn't require him to listen, so he didn't. Mas actually liked having a reason to get up early, like when he had dozens of customers six days a week. Now, because of his bad back and age, that number had dwindled to half a dozen. So it was actually nice to have some kind of purpose to rise before dawn, even if it happened to be serving as Haruo's chauffeur.

Haruo had gotten that job at the flower market a few years ago. He described himself as the right-hand man of Taxie, the manager of Freeway Flowers, but Mas knew that Haruo's title was closer to grunt. He wrapped flowers in newspaper, helped customers load up their vans and trucks, retrieved handcarts, swept the concrete floor, and bought coffee for the rest of the workers. It was honest and physical work, which Mas had hoped would keep him out of trouble. And so far it had.

The flower market was already going at full throttle at four o'clock in the morning, judging from the line of vans and trucks waiting by the parking kiosk. Most everything around the area was aging concrete — the public lots, the neighboring dives, and the flower market itself. It had been the belle of the ball in the 1960s, a sleek everything-under-one-roof building, the biggest of its kind perhaps in the world. But that's when people still grew flowers in places like Blue Hills, as East Whittier had

92

been called, and Dominguez, which, in its present-day incarnation as Compton, was known more for drive-by shootings than delphiniums. There was no flower growing now in Los Angeles County, aside from some holdouts in San Dimas and Palos Verdes, and, of course, nurseries that grew their plants underneath electrical towers.

Blooms were still sold in the flower market, but instead of carnations from Hawthorne and gladiolas from San Diego, the flowers were from towns in Colombia, Ecuador, Mexico, and Thailand. From the buyers' standpoint, a rose was a rose; it didn't matter whether it sunned itself in a greenhouse in Northern California or outside in a field in South America.

It was Mas's turn at the parking kiosk. Mas rolled down his window, and Haruo scooted over to the driver's side so far that he was almost sitting in Mas's lap.

"He just gonna drop me off, Johnny," he explained to the parking lot attendant.

"No, gonna park," Mas corrected Haruo. "Need to talk to somebody."

Haruo just seemed happy that Mas would be going into work with him, so he didn't ask why or whom he was planning to talk to. He navigated Mas through the covered lot to an empty spot between an old van and a shiny SUV.

After parking, Mas walked sideways in between the van and the Ford, only to discover a couple of alley cats meowing at them.

"Hallo." Haruo got down on his knees and greeted them like old friends. Before Mas could warn him not to, Haruo was scratching their chins and nuzzling the matted fur on their cheeks.

Mas grimaced. "No tellin' what kind of *byōki* those cats have."

"These cats so *kawaii,* how can they be sick?"

Mas spit on the concrete. Yah, cuteness can fool you, draw you in, and before you know it, it can even kill you. That was the case with old men and young girls. And, who knew, maybe with kittens.

"These *neko* work hard, you know? Catch a bunch of rats each day, most likely. I feedsu them ebery day before I go home."

"C'mon." Mas gestured to the entrance of the flower market. "Youzu gonna be late."

Punctuality for Mas and most men and women of his generation and background was paramount. There was no excuse for being late. Bad traffic, accident, death in the family, earthquake, even a police investigation — it didn't matter. The hands on the clock and digital numbers on a watch ruled their world.

They walked down an expansive hall, past offices for orchid traders, a wholesale florist supply center, a store selling pots, down the escalator onto the main floor, the air thick with a mixture of car exhaust and the fragrance of flowers. It was such a powerful punch that it almost set Mas back a few steps up the escalator. Haruo, on the other hand, had become immune to it. Whether it was bad or good, if you lived with the same thing day after day, your body just took it for granted.

Mas followed Haruo through a maze of open-air stalls. Signs with the number and name of each business dangled from above via linked chains. There were the greens man, with stalks of shiny banana leaves, furry ferns, and striped crotons; the tropical flower outfit with long boxes full of magenta dendrobrium leis and stalks of lobster claw heliconia; and a local grower of misshapen sunflowers and gypsophila, resembling a rain of dandruff.

Each stall had a different specialty and all were in a war — albeit a friendly one — with each other. Standing orders for regular customers had been bunched together hours earlier and were sitting in buckets of water. Florists and special events planners still trolled other stalls to see if any offerings struck their fancy. Many times it wasn't about only the beauty of their products but also their price. By the end of the morning, there were deals to be had because flowers weren't like cans of beans — they had a very limited shelf life, usually less than forty-eight hours.

As they turned the corner around some chrysanthemum growers from Carpinteria, Mas came face-to-face with just about the last female he wanted to see. She was wearing a white T-shirt and jeans and was casually leaning against a cart filled with pompon chrysanthemums. On her feet were old-fashioned Converse basketball high-tops, the kind that Mari used to wear. "I'm getting some new wheels soon," Mas couldn't help hear her boast to an Asian man in his forties.

Mas blocked Haruo from her view and told him to get the hell out of there. As Haruo slipped away to report to Freeway Flowers, Mas knew that he had to confront the Buckwheat Beauty. He stood right in front of her, his eyes reaching the top of her chin. "You gotsu it all wrong," he said.

The man she had been talking to became busy with a customer and Mas gave her no space to avoid him.

"Haruo didn't have nuttin' to do wiz those dolls," Mas declared.

Dee folded her arms. "Then why did he run in the opposite direction when he saw me right now? And why isn't he talking to the police?"

"Maybe he don't like being accuse. Youzu already tellsu police he did it. Now he gotta prove he didn't."

"Well, then who did? No locks were broken. Somebody most likely got in with a key. Haruo has one."

And you do too, Mas thought, staring into the Buckwheat Beauty's eyes. They were bloodshot and even tinged with yellow. These were a sick woman's eyes, an addict's eyes.

Before they could continue their verbal sparring, a woman wheeling some pots of hydrangea required them to move, effectively breaking up Mas and Dee like a referee in a boxing match. Dee went into her corner and made her getaway with her carts of pompons. *Good riddance,* Mas thought. *Run away, run away, Buckwheat Beauty.*

Mas searched for Haruo, but Taxie was the only one manning Freeway Flowers. He was talking to a man in a button-down shirt

97

and slacks. A leather case for his cell phone hung from his belt like a holster.

"Where's Haruo?"

"Went to get some coffee. Hey, Mas, I want to introduce you to somebody. Felipe Rodriguez, he owns the Rose Emporium down there. This is Mas Arai, you know, the one that Haruo always talks about."

"So you are that Mas?" Felipe's eyes grew big. His voice sounded heavy, and Mas could tell his native country was somewhere south of California. "Mas, Mas, Mas. More, more, more, yes, in my language?" He laughed, but Mas didn't understand what the man found funny.

"You have some time? Come, come see my flowers."

Mas had seen a lifetime's worth of flowers and had no desire to see more. But this Felipe was hard to refuse, so Mas agreed to stop by the Rose Emporium after he had a private word with Taxie.

"Police gonna call you to talk to Haruo," Mas whispered in his ear.

Taxie's mouth fell open. "Didn't know it was so serious. Weren't they only dolls that were taken?"

Mas nodded. "But these no regula dolls. Worth three thousand dolla."

Taxie looked as shocked as Mas. "And

98

they suspect Haruo?"

"Thanks to Dee Hayakawa. She tellsu police to watch out for him."

Taxie wrapped some gerber daisies in newspaper. "I don't know why she's been against Haruo ever since she came back to work here. Seems like she's jealous of him, like he was taking her mother away from her."

"Anyway, Haruo scared to talk to them right now. Cantcha send him down somewhere to clean out storage or sumptin'? At least until evertin' calm?"

Taxie looked conflicted. "Easter's coming up pretty soon, so I'll need him on the floor. But I'll see what I can do."

Two middle-aged women in T-shirts stood in front of Freeway Flowers carrying five dripping bouquets. Mas knew that this was his signal to leave and excused himself to take a tour of Rose Emporium.

Felipe Rodriguez's space was the size of three stalls. If the man's worth was based on the sheer number of his flowers, his bank account must be bursting at the seams.

"I opened up my business here in the eighties," Felipe explained. "Importing from Latin America. Colombia. It was when the United States gave Colombia money to grow flowers instead of drugs. One old-timer — I think he had spent some time in Japan — he called it —" Felipe rested his hand on his belt. "What's the Japanese word for flowers, again?"

"Hana."

"Yes, he called it the Hana War. The American flower growers were being attacked by Latin America. And then Southeast Asia. Imports were taking over. People here didn't want to let me into the flower market. Some folks like Taxie and others welcomed me. They knew Latin America was the future. In my country, flowers grow like weeds. You don't need fancy lighting equipment or expensive greenhouses. The climate is perfect. The flowers just grow under the sun. Beautiful."

Mas toured the flowers with his eyes. The stems were long and upright, the flower petals tight and unblemished. They were indeed impressive. Except for one thing — they didn't smell, perhaps due to strong chemicals used overseas. Mas preferred the gangly, insect-bitten roses, full of thorns, that weighed heavy on bushes in his customers' yards. In spite of their visual imperfection, they were full of scent.

"I've gotten used to Japanese Americans. One thing I know at least from the guys here is they don't BS. They don't like me, they don't deal with me. They like me, they give me free food."

Haruo poked his head in the stall. "Been lookin' for me?"

"Haruo, I've been talking to your friend," Felipe said.

Haruo smiled. "Hallo, Felipe," he said and turned his attention back to Mas. "*So-ka,* forgot to tell you, but G.I. and Juanita want to eat dinner early wiz us ova at Juanita's place. Taxie gonna drop me off. You can come, *deshō?*"

Before Mas could answer, someone else called out his name.

"Hey, Mas, whatchu doing here?" Casey Nakayama was originally from Hawaii, and one side of his lip was always swollen and limp as if a dentist had shot it up with too much novocaine. He was tall and he shuffled when he walked. He had been working for a flower grower for over forty years, and even though he was semiretired, he kept coming to the market. Subterranean life suited him, Mas guessed.

"Had to drive Haruo ova. Heezu living' wiz me." Mas turned to where Haruo had been standing, but he had mysteriously disappeared.

"What about a round of liar's poker? A bunch of us play on our break at ten in the supply department."

Liar's poker wasn't played with cards but with the serial numbers on dollar bills. It was kid stuff, but it was an opportunity to dig out what was really going on behind the scenes. Gambling, even liar's poker, often brought out the truth in Mas's circles. So he readily agreed.

Promptly at ten, Mas went into a separate room called the supply department. Up front was a display of florists' tape, Styrofoam cylinders and cones of different sizes, plastic and glass vases, metal wire, and baskets.

"Glad you were able to make it," Casey said, his fingers wrapped around an unlit cigarette. There was no smoking in the flower market, but having tobacco close by comforted any addict. Mas followed Casey past the cabinets to a storage area filled with giant boxes that could easily hold a body of a man Mas's size. Casey gestured toward a folding table and chairs next to the door. Mas sat down.

"Neva knew about this place back here," Mas said.

"Well, it's either here or the dungeon."

Mas scrunched up his nose.

"The dungeon's over by the coffeehouse. Secret little room where the rats live. We chose here instead." He explained that the police had been making their rounds in the market, so there was reason to be careful. He eased himself in a seat across from Mas. "Noticed you were talkin' to the Hayakawa girl."

Mas nodded.

"She's trouble. Always has been. Spoon's been crying her eyes out over that one."

At that point, two men appeared from behind some boxes. Casey made the introductions: The short man from El Salvador was Roberto, who had just started working there, and a *hakujin* man, Pete, was a veteran. "We call him Pico," explained Casey. "And Roberto doesn't speak much English."

Mas hated silly nicknames, especially those that made no sense. A white man named Pico? Okay, he'd go along because he didn't have much of a choice. Roberto and Pico claimed the two other seats.

"Haruo want in?" Pico asked. Even though the hair on his head was graying, his five o'clock shadow was the color of old pennies.

"He quit gambling, remember?" Casey said.

"Oh, yeah, I re-mem-ber." Pico drew out his syllables like stretching taffy and Mas grew suspicious. What did Pico know? Was

103

that behind Haruo's sudden disappearing act — that he feared his dubious gambling associations may be revealed by Casey?

"Everyone ready?" Casey asked. They nodded simultaneously and pulled out dollar bills from their wallets. Mas had to pull out his reading glasses to read the number of his bill. It was in green ink on the side of George Washington's face: 65994144. A pair of nines and three fours. In front of his number was the letter *L*.

Roberto had the lowest letter, *G,* so he started things off. After reminding everyone that 1 was an ace and 0 was a 10, he said, "*Tres* sixes."

"Three eights," said Casey.

"Four twos," said Pico.

Whatthehell, Mas thought. Liar's poker was all about lying. "Four threes."

Roberto paused for a second, a second too long for Mas's taste. "*Cuatro cuatros.*"

Casey had picked up on Roberto's hesitation. "Challenge," he said.

"Challenge," said Pico.

"Challenge," Mas echoed.

Roberto cursed in Spanish and showed his bill. Only one four.

They found another bill in their wallets and started the betting all over again.

"That's too bad about Haruo and Spoon,

huh?" said Casey.

"What do you mean?" Pico seemed curious.

"They split up."

"No kiddin'."

"Yah, Mas will tell you all about it. You were supposed to be the best man, right?"

Mas shrugged his shoulders. "Yah, suppose to be. But some trouble." The minute Mas mentioned "trouble," he regretted it. In a pool of sharks, "trouble" was fresh blood.

"What kind of trouble, anyhow?" asked Pico. "Heard that Haruo stole something of Spoon's to feed his gambling addiction."

"Haruo didn't steal nuttin'. Just some dolls gone missin'."

"Dolls?" Pico asked.

"Doesn't seem worth calling off a wedding for dolls."

"Those special Japanese dolls. *Hina* dolls."

"Sounds like collector's items," said Casey.

"Yah, police may be comin' by. If you see them, let Taxie know, *orai?*"

"Police," Casey murmured. He was clutching his dollar bill so hard that it was starting to crinkle on one side.

"Those dollsu belong to Spoon's husband. The first one, I meansu."

The storage room grew quiet and Mas felt the oppressiveness of the stacks of boxes surrounding them.

"Casey doesn't like talking about Ike Hayakawa, and especially the de Groots."

Mas lowered his dollar bill. What was Pico saying?

"Shaddap, Pico." Casey's lisp seemed to become more evident under stress.

"Well, ever since Geoff de Groot tossed you out of his father's funeral."

"Shaddap, Pico!"

Pico seemed wounded by Casey's sharp tongue and pulled his dollar bills from the table. "Gotta go back to work," he announced and left the supply department. Roberto followed a few moments later.

Casey, however, stayed behind. Kicking the concrete floor with his size-ten feet, he cursed. "That damn Pico. Always flapping his trap."

Mas remained seated, tracing a torn section of the card table's vinyl top with a dirty fingernail.

"I wasn't the one who did anything wrong. It was Jorg and Ike."

Mas leaned back in his chair until he felt the edge of a box press against his head.

"Cocaine," whispered Casey. "That's why Jorg and Ike got killed. It was a Mexican mob hit. Jorg was running around with a lot of money. Stone-cold cash. I saw it with my own eyes. I was helping Jorg and his son Geoff unload his truck of some birds-of-paradise and then a bag fell out onto the floor. Stacks of new twenties. Jorg made some excuse, that he hadn't been able to make a run to the bank, but I didn't believe him. When those two got killed in Hanley, I knew the truth. It was no accident."

Mas slowly blew out some air from his cheeks.

"I didn't tell police. I didn't tell the insurance companies. I kept my mouth shut. But because Geoff knows that I know, he's punished me all these years."

"Insurance?"

"You didn't hear? Those two guys each bought one-million-dollar life insurance policies on themselves. What flower grower's going to do that? Spoon breaking off the engagement with Haruo is the best thing to happen to him, believe me. The Hayakawas and de Groots are bad news, I'm telling you. I know that Haruo is your friend, so you should tell him to thank his lucky stars that the wedding got called off." With that, Casey stomped out of the storage room with his meager winnings.

Mas also claimed his dollar bills on the

table. If Casey's intent was to scare Mas, he'd succeeded. Television shows and movies domesticated the Italian mob and even Japanese gangsters, but Mas knew the reality was very different.

He did not have straight-out dealings with the yakuza in Japan, but he had plenty of contact with the *chinpira,* lowlife gangsters who had multiplied like mold after World War Two. They were the masters of the black market, two-bit gambling, *hiropon,* and alcohol made from weak gasoline.

These *chinpira* had entrapped a young girl Mas had met after the war, an orphan who had lost her parents in the bombing, into a life of prostitution. These gangsters weren't that scary, but fierce enough to send not a few innocents down a path of destruction.

The problem with gangsters was that they were close to impossible to exterminate. You tried to crush one, and four emerged in his place. If Ike and Jorg were playing around with the Mexican Mafia, it was no surprise that they got burned and burned for good. Mas would have to watch himself or else his own fingers would get singed.

Mas was back on the freeway, this time to the home of his Alhambra customer. Dr. Svelick had been Mas's customer for the past seven years. Mas had watched him grow from a young resident, stopping by the house at odd times in green scrubs, to a full-fledged private practitioner who wore a tie five days a week. Mas knew that one day the doctor, who was starting to go *ohage* around the back of his head like an old-fashioned Catholic priest, would someday move to a more upscale neighborhood like San Marino. But for now Mas had him and he would relish the working relationship. The doctor never complained and mailed in his monthly check like clockwork. No *monku* and money you can count on. What else could a gardener past his prime ask for?

The traffic on the 10 was still moving at a crawl and Mas couldn't help but to think of the two dead men who had been buddy-buddy. What would possess seemingly straight-arrow guys like Jorge de Groot and Ike Hayakawa to do something illegal? The two men, with their sturdy middle-class ranch homes in the suburbs, obviously seemed to be able to support their families with legitimate work. Why did Casey want to tarnish their reputations by spreading rumors after both were long gone?

Mas finally reached the off-ramp for Dr. Svelick's house and went north on Fremont. Construction delayed him further, so by the time he turned onto the doctor's street, Mas was ready to hop out of the truck and get to work. Except that another gardener's truck was parked in front of Dr. Svelick's. It was a white Toyota, probably about twenty years old but maintained as if it were a newborn. The hubcaps had been replaced with shiny racing ones, and the back of the bed, which at one time sported the brand name TOYOTA, now read just YO.

Mas frowned and parked in back of the revamped truck. His stomach felt queasy. He had a bad feeling about this.

As he approached the doctor's home, the side back door swung open and Mas heard the banter of Spanish and then saw a couple of men carrying a gardener's catcher full of freshly mowed grass. The smell of the grass was powerful, pungent — no matter how many lawns Mas had cut, that scent gave him a high no drug could. The second man, donning a worn wide-brimmed straw hat shaped like an upside-down Chinese teacup, abruptly stopped in his tracks upon noticing Mas. He was tall and brown and somehow looked familiar. He had a strong profile, narrow face, and high-ridged nose.

"Hello, Mister." The boy took off his straw hat and smiled widely. "Remember me?"

It was the sardonic grin that helped place

the face. Mas's former helper Eduardo's nephew. This was the same boy who refused to get into his truck because it was too old. How long had it been? At least six, seven years.

"Dr. Svelick give this to you." The boy handed Mas a neat white envelope.

Mas didn't have to open it to know what it was. Sometimes the message came via the telephone, sometimes in a thin envelope like this one, mailed to the house. Either way, the communication was short and to the point: "We won't be needing your services anymore."

To have the message delivered by his replacement was especially cruel and humiliating indeed. And this one — a boy probably barely in his twenties! A youngster who had disparaged Mas's beloved Ford once upon a time.

Mas edged closer to Eduardo's nephew, and the young man must have detected Mas's foul mood because he took a few steps back. "Whatchu name?" Mas asked.

"Raul Jesus," the boy replied, pronouncing his second name the traditional Spanish way: hey-sus.

Jesus. That just plain figured. Thanks or perhaps no thanks to Tug, Mas was starting to open his heart to God, and this is what

He gives him? That's why *bachi,* what goes around comes around, had once seemed to make more sense to Mas. Either God didn't exist or He had a very mean streak in Him.

Mas was going to tear up the envelope and throw it at Raul Jesus like confetti, but he thought better of it. There was probably a final check in there, and in these lean economic times, Mas had to put his emotion aside, at least for this week. There was no telling how long Haruo would be staying at the house, for example, and Mas might need that money to set his friend up with a deposit on a new apartment.

"Raul Gee-sus, good luck to youzu," Mas growled and turned on the heels of his scuffed work boots and marched back to the Ford. He was so mad that he even entertained the thought of dragging his key along the span of the perfectly hospital-white side panel of the Toyota. Only for a second, however. No decent man would ever deface another man's automobile. Some things were sacred; that line should not be crossed.

Once Mas hopped into the Ford, he squeezed the steering wheel so tight that his joints hurt. How in the world could this Raul Jesus have stolen Dr. Svelick from him? And then he remembered. When he was laid up around Christmas with shingles, he had called Eduardo to cover for him. He must have brought along his nephew, this Jesus. It was then that the takeover plan had been set in motion. There was no doubt that the boy must be charging at least twenty percent less than Mas's standard rate. *Inu!* Traitors, all of them.

It was only when Mas was a good three blocks away that he had the nerve to open the envelope while he was stopped at an intersection. The note was written in Dr. Svelick's lopsided scrawl. Mas couldn't make out all of the words, but the last paragraph was fairly readable: "I've appreciated your hard work for me over the years. Just think it's best — for both you and me — that we make this change. You really deserve to take it easy. Enjoy your life!"

CHAPTER SIX

Odairisama to ohinasama
Futari narande sumashikao
Oyome ni irashita nēsamani
Yokunita kanjōno shiroikao

Emperor and empress
Side by side, grave expressions
At the wedding are maidens
Their white faces all alike
— "Hina Matsuri Song," second stanza

"Enjoy my life!" Mas muttered as he drove to Juanita Gushiken's family's Japanese-Peruvian restaurant on Virgil in Los Angeles. He couldn't get Dr. Svelick's breezy directive out of his head. The mantra had played in his head all afternoon. *Enjoymylife!* Driving home to his sidewalkless neighborhood in Altadena. *Enjoymylife!* Splashing water on his face and combing his hair back with Three Flowers oil. *Enjoymylife!* Fooling with the lock of the Ford as the screwdriver technique wasn't working effectively.

If he was to enjoy his life, he might as well do it at the Peruvian Palace. Unlike its royal name, the eatery, located a couple of doors down from a Laundromat, was no frills. No frills meant no carpet and no tablecloths, just scuffed-up linoleum and paper napkins from a metal dispenser. But the food was tasty. Mas's favorite was the fresh mound of seafood ceviche — baby octopus legs tangled through circles of squid and topped with orange-striped unshelled shrimp.

Mas opened the tinted glass door and spied G.I. Hasuike, Juanita's boyfriend, seated in their usual spot, a corner booth.

"Eh, Mas, long time," said G.I., finishing off a sip of Inca Kola.

It *had* been a long time. Long enough for G.I. to have chopped off his salt-and-pepper waist-long horse tail. In fact, the fiftysomething man had taken a razor to his head and now resembled a crazed skinny monk who had stayed in the monastery too long. Mas had actually met G.I. through Wishbone when a young Japanese acquaintance was knee-deep in legal problems. Ever since then, G.I. was usually the first person Mas called when he needed help from a Sansei, third-generation Japanese American, with a

115

JD degree.

Juanita, wearing an apron, waved from the other side of the room. A Japanese Peruvian with roots in Okinawa, she was a PI by day and a dutiful daughter by night. When G.I.'s friend was found stabbed to death in a Hawaiian restaurant, Mas and Juanita joined forces to discover the truth behind a clue remaining at the crime scene, an Okinawan stringed instrument called a snakeskin *shamisen*.

"Haruo called. He's running a little late but says to start," Juanita announced, placing plates of soft rolls and green sauce in the middle of their table. Mas knew enough not to soak the roll in the sauce. It was like wasabi — a few drops gave starch some needed kick, but any more sent you to guzzle down a gallon of water and maybe to the bathroom as well.

He ordered a beer and Juanita left to get a bottle from a refrigerator near the counter.

"So, too bad about Haruo, huh?" G.I. said.

"Heezu comin' tonight."

G.I. nodded. "How is he?"

Mas shrugged. "Stayin' at my place."

G.I. began to cough, almost choking on his roll. Then his whole body shook with laughter. After taking a last drink of his Inca

116

Kola, he asked, "And how's that working out for you, Mas?"

After delivering Mas's beer, Juanita sat with the two men in the booth. Although she was lean and muscular, she was all female inside. She wanted to know all the details of what Spoon had said to Haruo (Mas didn't know), how Haruo was taking it (pretty good), and how much money was lost in canceling the wedding (Mas had no idea). Once the fortysomething woman had pumped as much information about Haruo and Spoon's relationship as she could — extracting only about a cupful of useful gossip — she put on her private investigator cap and began asking about the theft of the dolls. G.I., whose eyes were starting to glaze over, seemed to be reinvigorated. A lawyer who lived on the fumes of conflict, G.I. was always attracted to anything related to crime.

"You know much about Mexican gangsters?" Mas abruptly asked.

Juanita glanced at G.I. "Well, there's the Eighteenth Street gang, which started back in L.A. in the sixties. You're not getting involved with them, are you? They are very dangerous, Mas."

"Howsuabout cocaine? Whatchu knowsu

about cocaine?"

"Cocaine, Mas? What is all this about?"

Mas shared what he'd learned from Casey, not revealing his name, of course. Casey had shared in the heat of anger to protect his reputation and it wasn't fair to hold that against him.

"Well, cocaine was big in the eighties, very big. That time was the powdered kind that rich people used," G.I. said. "And what followed that was crack cocaine. You know, you smoke it in a pipe." G.I. seemed to know his share about *mayaku* and Mas guessed that some of that knowledge was firsthand experience. Turned out his hunch was right.

"A lot of us got involved in drugs in the seventies and eighties, Mas. It's just that some of us couldn't leave it."

Juanita nodded. She was a decade younger than G.I. but apparently old enough to have lived through that time herself.

"Asian American groups like the Yellow Brotherhood came in to help addicts. We were losing too many people to cocaine." From this effort came drug abuse recovery centers, which were in existence even today, according to G.I.

"Datsu what happen to Spoon's daughter." Rehab, isn't that what Haruo called it?

"What's her name?" asked G.I.

118

"Dee Hayakawa."

"Sounds familiar. She from the Eastside?"

"Montebello."

"Well, generally speaking, I didn't really hang out with any girls from Montebello. Those were the rich girls."

Even though Mas didn't think Ike and Spoon were especially wealthy, anything compared to East L.A., where G.I. was from, had to be considered rich, he guessed. The two communities were separated by only a few miles, but it might as well have been two kingdoms, for how the neighborhoods were different.

"So, this Dee is staying with Spoon?" G.I. asked.

Mas nodded.

"That's tough," commented Juanita. "I mean, I can see why Spoon would want to help her daughter out, but sometimes people in trouble need to hit rock bottom."

Mas knew that those things were easy for Juanita to say but hard to do. Wasn't she herself living in the back house on her parents' property? Juanita and her Peruvian immigrant parents were close, as close as an adult child and parents could be.

"Anotha thing kinda don't make sense. The *hina* dolls. Spoon tell me they cost four

119

hundred, but now it look like three thousand."

"Three thousand?" G.I. opened his mouth wide, showing off the metal fillings on his molars.

"I thought that Spoon didn't have any money," Juanita added.

"Yah, datsu what Haruo say. But she got one million from husband's insurance policy. What happen to dat?"

"Four hundred." G.I. ignored Mas's question and returned to the sum that Spoon reported to the police. "That's interesting. You know four hundred is the limit between a felony and misdemeanor."

So what, Spoon was trying to protect Haruo?

G.I. continued with his train of thought. "But how would Spoon know that? She doesn't seem the type to be savvy about the judicial process. And it's not like she's ever been arrested for grand theft."

A face full of freckles surfaced in Mas's mind. The Buckwheat Beauty. He could only imagine what trouble she had gotten into in the past.

"Haruo needsu your helpu," said Mas regarding G.I.'s legal expertise.

G.I. rubbed his shaved head. "I offered it to him, or at least some good referrals of public defenders. He told me that it hadn't gotten that far yet. But it definitely didn't sound like he was planning to go to the police on his own. Why is he so reluctant? Usually Haruo is the first in line to talk to anyone."

Before Mas could answer, he saw Juanita smiling at a figure walking toward them.

"Haruo," she said. "So good to see you."

Haruo, however, did not seem happy to be there. His keloid scar, twisted like an old wisteria stem, was pulsating with anger. He didn't acknowledge Juanita and G.I.; all his attention was on Mas. "Why you go —" He had to pause to catch his breath. "Why you go," he restarted, "ova to place where Spoon buy her dollsu without tellin' me?"

Mas didn't know what to say.

"The place in San Diego callsu her, wonderin' why dis Mas Arai askin' all these questions."

Juanita shifted uncomfortably in her seat and G.I. gazed down at his soda can. Mas was being played as an interfering spy and there was probably no convincing Haruo otherwise. But Mas had to at least try.

"Izu just tryin' to helpu," Mas attempted to say as confidently as possible. "Dunno whyzu Spoon so upset."

"Well, sheezu mad. Sayin' dis none of your

121

bizness. Yell at me right in the middle of market. Youzu always say mind my bizness, but you don't mind yours."

Here you are, living at my place, eating all my instant ramen, Mas wanted to shout, but he bit his tongue. If he went there, there would be no turning back.

"Whyzu you go there and say nuttin' to me?" Haruo repeated.

Because I don't trust your former fiancée, Mas said to himself. *And I don't trust the daughter of your former fiancée.*

"I just wanna find out whatsu behind those dolls. And whatchu say to her? I think youzu say sumptin' mean, sumptin' dat make her cry."

At this point Mas was so frustrated that he didn't show any restraint. "I tole her dat she shoulda say to you plain and square she don't wanna get married." As soon as Mas spoke those words, he regretted it, as Haruo almost shook from the pain of it.

"Why don't we eat?" Juanita said brightly, but both Mas and Haruo could tell her smile was pasted on just for show.

"Not hungry," Haruo said.

"Me neither," Mas said, his stomach growling.

"I gonna just wait outside," Haruo said and turned back toward the door.

"Wait," Juanita called out, but even she was unable to stop him.

Mas shrugged his shoulders and got up. At least it would be a quiet ride home, he tried to tell himself, but it was a loud kind of silence that bothered Mas's ears more than Haruo's actual jabbering.

How come you bother my ex-fiancée? the silence said. *Why you snooping around?*

I'm just trying to help you, Mas said without words. *Don't want you to be thrown in jail. Don't want you getting into gambling again. I've had to pick you up time and time again. I'm through with that now.*

Of course, neither of them verbalized his thoughts. Words required too much energy and they also offered resolution. With silence, they could let their feud go on without an end. If Haruo wanted to play it that way, then Mas would abide.

Haruo finally ended his silent treatment at about ten o'clock. Three hours of silence was a record for him. "I gonna move out in a coupla days," he announced.

How was he going to find the money for a deposit and decent place? Mas wondered. But although Mas didn't give Haruo any credit, he knew that his friend did have a sprinkling of pride. It would be wrong to take that little of it away.

■ ■ ■ ■

That night Mas sank into a fitful sleep, waking up a couple times after some nightmares, including one starring a late customer, Mrs. Zidle. She was crying at the doorway of her Southern-style white wood-framed house in Pasadena. She was making a harsh, choking sound, like a cat coughing up a hairball. Her papery cheeks were wet and tears dripped from her chin.

He did get out of bed once at around four. He stumbled in the dark to get to the living room, and as he suspected, the couch that Haruo was using as his bed was empty. Haruo had found his own way to work, which was just fine for Mas. *None of my business, right?* he told himself. He collapsed back in bed and, this time, really slept until he was awakened by the ringing of the phone. Digital clock: 9:29 A.M.

"Hallo," Mas answered loudly, half looking forward to hanging up rudely on a telemarketer.

"Mas? It's Genessee Howard."

"Oh, hallo." Mas sat up and patted down his hair, as if doing those things would make a better impression on someone on the other end of the line.

"What happened on Sunday?"

"Huh?"

"Haruo and Spoon's wedding. I went to the Japanese garden and some people said the ceremony was canceled."

"Haruo didn't call you?" Mas was glad to silently curse Haruo. Genessee Howard should have been the first person on Haruo's to-call list. At least she would have been on Mas's.

"Oh, sorry. So sorry." Mas tried the best he could to piece together what had transpired between Haruo and Spoon — without revealing anything too personal or criminal.

"I'm sad to hear about that. You figure that love the second time around would be a lot easier."

Mas's cheeks grew cold. He didn't have the nerve to respond.

Thankfully Genessee continued talking. "Well, now that I have you on the phone, I was wondering if you could come by my house sometime. I bought my son's house in L.A. and it needs a lot of work. I know that you're just working part time, but I need some gardening advice."

"I come right now." Today Mas had only one customer, practically a mow and blow that he could do with his eyes closed.

"This morning? You're not busy?"

"Not so much." No sense in putting up a fake front. Besides, it would be good to get away from the conflict with Haruo.

"Okay," said Genessee. "Looking forward to seeing you."

"Yah."

Mas hung up the phone. He remembered holding Genessee's hand when they were all over at Mas's friend Tug's house. Tug was one of those true-blue Christians who said grace before a meal and wanted everyone to link hands around the table. Normally Mas wasn't too crazy about holding someone else's hand, but Genessee was an exception that he was more than willing to make.

When Mas had first met Genessee Howard, she was living smack-dab in the middle of the Japanese American community in Torrance. An expert in Okinawan music, she was the one Juanita Gushiken called to find out about the history of the *shamisen,* a clue in the death of G.I.'s Vietnam War veteran friend. Mas was first puzzled by her, then intrigued, and finally smitten. It was as if the very best of Chizuko had been boiled down and re-formed in this sixtysomething woman.

Genessee now lived in a neighborhood called Mid-City, but for Mas, who traveled mostly around the San Gabriel Valley, it might as well have been the Midwest. It was Los Angeles, for sure, but within L.A., nestled beside landmarks like Hollywood, Silver Lake, Crenshaw, Gallegos Park, and Watts, were lesser-known communities such as Hermon, Carthay, Chesterfield Square, and Harvard Heights. These were the places that, if mentioned on the television news, would cause someone like Mas to scratch his head and say to himself, "Where's that?"

Mid-City was in the middle of the line going from downtown Los Angeles to Santa Monica due west. It seemed like a good-enough neighborhood, neither very poor nor very rich. As Mas drove through the streets, he noticed that each house was unique, the lawns well tended. One home was painted purple with dark succulents planted all over. A gargoyle statue sat on the edge of the roof. Another home, framed by a natural wood gateway, was dotted with brilliant wildflowers. The front yard was filled with sparkly broken granite rocks. Judging by the way the inhabitants decorated the exterior of their homes, Mid-City attracted its share of *kawarimono,* eccentrics who didn't toe the line. There was obviously nothing midway about Mid-City.

Mas turned the corner onto Genessee's street. There was a gardener's truck parked across the street, and as Mas passed by, he was surprised to see an elderly black gardener in a jumpsuit and pith helmet loading a lawn mower in the back of the cab. He was joined by two younger gardeners in the same color jumpsuits — perhaps the elder's sons? Mas hadn't seen a black gardener in L.A. since the fifties, and to see three of them at one time was jarring indeed.

Genessee was waiting for him. Wearing an orange dress and yellow sweater, she sat on a bench on her porch and Mas couldn't help but smile inside. Her hair was combed out in a small Afro, different from the last time Mas had seen her. Her Asian eyes, bright behind her glasses, seemed aware of every movement on her quiet street.

"Hello," she said, as Mas parked the truck. He didn't bother to lock it, because what was worth taking? Anyway, he wanted to leave his key, the screwdriver, on the front seat. He wanted to try something new and look dignified for once.

Mas started to nod his head as a greeting, but Genessee wouldn't have it. She walked up to him and hugged him briefly. Mas stiffened as he felt her shoulder blades

128

against his palms.

"It's been a long time."

"Yah," Mas said. It had actually been around seven months, but who was counting?

"You look well."

Mas nodded. "Same to you."

Genessee smiled, her cheeks full of air, as if she were trying to swallow a laugh, and Mas wondered why. "Would you like to see my new backyard?" she finally asked.

Mas followed Genessee down a narrow walkway and into a small yard. Mas was prepared for something flat, as was typical of the backyards he saw in the congested Westside. But instead he encountered two twin dirt mounds.

"My grandson created that when he was into motocross racing. Before that, my son dug up the backyard to create a lagoon. But now I want to make this space just for me. I'm thinking of maybe a koi pond."

Mas chose to keep his thoughts to himself until he at least heard the woman out. Everyone in California seemed koi crazy, but they never thought about the downsides.

"When I last visited my relatives in Okinawa, they had this marvelous koi pond in the middle of their house. Well, it wasn't literally in the middle of their house, but the house wrapped around it."

Genessee, whose mother was Okinawan and father was black, was obviously trying to bring Japan to America. But attempting to plant Japan overseas sometimes didn't work out that well.

"Umm. Koi pond, *ne.*"

"You don't think it's a good idea." Genessee was able to quickly read Mas's face, a skill that Mas appreciated.

"Animals outside getsu hungry, you know. Ova in Altadena, we gotsu put chicken wire all ova. The raccoons like koi."

Genessee nodded. "We don't have that many raccoons, but I've smelled my share of skunks. One of my neighbors runs into possums all the time. Nasty creatures." She sucked in some air through her lips. "Maybe a koi pond wouldn't be such a good idea."

"I make youzu a rock garden," Mas declared.

"A rock garden." Genessee looked disoriented for a moment.

"Small round ones, smooth all ova. And maybe a couple of big ones too."

"I think I've seen a few in Japan. And maybe in photos."

Mas let the concept sink in with Genessee. Americans were often in love with bright colors and gaudiness. They didn't

130

quite understand *shibui,* restraint, the celebration of nothing balanced against something. It was hard to explain; it had to be felt. And Mas thought that if anyone could feel it, Genessee, the lover and scholar of Okinawan music, would be the one.

"Rocks, huh?"

"Hard to getsu. Used to be easy, we go to Los Angeles River. Against the law now."

"It won't look like that hideous granite lawn down the street."

Mas shook his head. "Dis one natural."

"Natural," Genessee said, rolling the word around in her head. "I like that."

After touring the backyard, Genessee invited Mas in for a cup of coffee in her kitchen. Truth be told, he should have been on his way to his customer back in San Gabriel, but one cup of coffee? What could that hurt?

He sat at Genessee's oak table. There seemed to be something reverent about it, so Mas removed his cap and placed it on an empty seat. He hoped that the top of his head wasn't fluffed up like a rooster's crown.

Genessee served her coffee strong in thick homemade mugs the color of red clay. Mas liked the rough feel of the handle in his hands.

"I made that," she announced unabashedly and with pride.

"*Hontō?*"

Genessee laughed. "Yes, really. It's so good to hear some Japanese. I miss hearing that from my mom and other old-timers."

Mas didn't know if that meant Genessee looked at him as a father figure, but she quickly squeezed his upper arm.

"I didn't mean that the way it came out. Just that it felt . . . what's that word — *natsu wa —*"

Mas frowned, then grinned. "*Natsukashii.*"

"Yes, *natsu—*" she continued to stumble over the word. "Nostalgic, right?"

Mas nodded and they talked some more, about how she had attended American school in Okinawa, so she was raised more American than Okinawan. She moved on to the present and explained that she was thinking of retiring from teaching at UCLA. Academia, she said, had changed so much. The students had changed. She wanted to spend her time making ceramic pots and drinking coffee outside in her new rock garden.

Mas nodded. He didn't insert any *aizuchi,* any "ah, *sodesuka,*" "*hai,*" "um," or "yah." He didn't have to give any verbal cues that he was listening, because it was obvious that he was soaking up every word. When Genessee seemed to have finished telling her story — at least for that day — Mas still didn't want to go. So he began to share as well. About the dream he had to be an automobile engineer but fell into gardening because for a Japanese American man who couldn't speak English too well, it was the thing to do. About the worry he carried for his daughter, Mari, even though she was close to being middle-aged. And finally, he couldn't help going into what had happened recently with Haruo and Spoon and the theft of the *hina* dolls. Genessee, who appreciated antiques, was especially intrigued with the dolls. "Do Japanese Americans still put them out?" she asked.

"Some," Mas said, explaining that his family never did. He seemed to remember one gardener friend with a lot of family *hokori* who did display dolls every March. "Those guys full of pride."

"Well, pride's not necessarily all bad, Mas."

He wasn't quite sure what Spoon's intention was in her acquisition of her husband's family dolls. But he didn't care, at least that's what he told Genessee. "Dat Spoon, she took Haruo for a big ride. And three thousand dolla, how come she lie about payin' dat much for those dollsu?" Bitterness seeped into his voice. Apparently Genessee wasn't a fan of bitterness, especially the kind directed at an old woman, because it was her turn to fall silent. Mas brought the homemade mug to his lips even though the coffee was long gone.

"You know, Mas, I think that you have to cut Spoon a break," Genessee finally said. "I think you're being too tough on her."

Mas hoped the heat rising to his cheeks was not noticeable.

"I don't agree with what she's doing to Haruo and I know that you're so close to Haruo, so I laud your loyalty. But there are two sides to the story. I don't know Spoon well, but I did get a chance to speak to her at that dinner at Tug's last year. She happened to mention her late husband. They were very close, it seemed."

"Heezu gone more than twenty years."

"But Mas, you never forget. You can't tell me that you don't think about your wife."

To hear the word "wife" from Genessee made Mas's heart grow cold. He pictured Chizuko's piercing stare. What would she be thinking if she were watching Mas now?

"I think of my husband often. Sometimes I even forget that he's gone. I think, *I need to tell Paul this story.* And then it dawns on me, he's dead."

Mas could relate to that confusion. One day in a customer's backyard he noticed that the fig tree was filled with ripe fruit. Figs weren't well liked by his customer, nor even Mas, for that matter, but were Chizuko's favorite. Mas considered pocketing some to take home before realizing that Chizuko would not be there to enjoy them.

"The wedding planning must have brought up some old memories of Spoon's first marriage. Do you know if she had a fancy ceremony?"

"Camp mess hall, I think. Manzanar."

"Of course, of course." Genessee fingered the lip of her mug. "Well, they got together during a sensitive time in their lives. The memories must be very deep. And those dolls, they must have been very precious to the family."

Mas didn't even consider any of that but understood how a person could be blind-sided by the past. Like old monster movies that used to be shown on weekend afternoon television, buried bodies sometimes wormed out of the ground when you least expected it.

"Mas, the mind and heart are very mysterious. It's like holding water. It's tight in your fist, but when you open up your hand, it's all gone."

135

Mas grunted and then glanced at his Casio. Already past eleven. He'd hoped to finish his customer by noon, but that wasn't going to happen today. Palms on the table, he pushed himself to his feet. "I gotta go."

"Oh, yes, it's already late," Genessee said. Did Mas actually detect a glimmer of disappointment in her eyes?

"Thanks so much for the coffee," Mas said. "Best I eva had."

Genessee shook her head, insisting that Mas was ōgesa, a master exaggerator, but he was telling the truth. It wasn't only the taste of the coffee, but the whole experience of drinking it in a vessel Genessee had made herself. Sure, Chizuko's Yuban version had been tasty as well, but she served hers in factory-made mugs that usually had something quite unseasonal on them like reindeer and snow during the heat of summer.

Mas stood by the door, the cap in his hand.

"You'll call me, then?" Genessee said. "I mean about the rock garden. All natural, right?"

Getting back on the 10, Mas wondered if his head was completely kara, empty of any brains. Genessee was interested only in his so-called expertise in gardening, nothing to do with him as a person or as a man. Then why did her hands seem warm and moist when she squeezed his elbow good-bye? There had been a spark — Mas was sure of it. That's when he came to the conclusion that he was close to losing his mind.

It was high noon as Mas arrived at his customer's house, just south of the San Gabriel Country Club and not far from the San Gabriel Mission, six bells hanging from its aging wall.

The job was easy, just a postage stamp of Saint Augustine grass. Despite its small size, the yard still managed to do the trick of sweating some of Mas's anger away. Mas was short-tempered, even back in the days with his seven brothers and sisters in Hiroshima. His temper always seemed to get the best of him, and as he grew older, he thought that his fuse had gotten much longer only to find himself spontaneously combusting when a certain button was pressed.

He found an old towel in back of his seat and wiped the sweat pooling in front of his ears. Removing his cap, he gave his whole face a good rub, tasting some remnants of lawn mower oil from the towel.

Genessee's words softened him. Had he been too hard on Spoon? He knew, perhaps

137

more than anyone alive (well, maybe Haruo's first wife, Yasuko, might know even better), what a mess Haruo actually was. Could Mas really blame Spoon for having doubts about Haruo? Marriage at their age literally meant "until death do us part." Here he was complaining about Haruo staying a couple of weeks at his place, and Spoon was facing a life sentence.

Mas realized that he had indeed said too much to Spoon. Maybe he should have minded his own business and not gone to Hina House. He had to offer something of an apology to her. So he headed over to Montebello, picking up a six-pack of Coca-Cola and, as a bonus, a can of cashews from a local liquor store. If this didn't say, "I'm sorry," Mas didn't know what did.

But at Spoon's, no one seemed to be in, no cars in the driveway. In fact, Spoon's whole street seemed dead quiet. These days in the Los Angeles suburbs robbers came to visit in broad daylight because, like on this street in Montebello, everyone was out working or running errands. Mas learned his lesson the last time and stayed put in the truck and waited. It was still spring and in the seventies, but Mas rolled down the window just for good measure.

He soon fell asleep and began to stir only

when he thought he heard something out-side. His face was smack against the banana-yellow passenger seat, his cheek wet with drool. He sat up and wiped his face with the back of his wrist. Sure enough, the sound of glass breaking. He got out of the truck and was in the middle of the street when a silver Oldsmobile Cutlass sped dangerously by him, almost clipping the monster side mirror he and Tug had in-stalled. The Oldsmobile veered into the neighbor's driveway and screeched to a stop. Out of the car appeared that woman with the crazy bird's nest hair. It wouldn't do to have someone call the police again, so Mas attempted to explain himself.

"Hey you," he called out.

The lady ran toward the back door.

Sonafugun, Mas muttered to himself. What kind of jumpy woman was this? He thought better of pursuing her. Forget about it. Mas needed to hightail it out of there before Officers Gallegos and Chang made their way over. Mas hadn't even reached the Ford when he heard a high-pitched shriek coming from her house. Mas ran toward the house and up the front steps, only to have the door fly open with two men in ski masks heading right toward him.

CHAPTER SEVEN

Reflexively, Mas closed his eyes for a second. He knew that in self-defense closing one's eyes didn't make much sense at all. You needed to face and clearly assess your opponent, both his weaknesses and strengths. But under Mas's skin was that forever experience, when the skies turned black and his eardrums felt like they were exploding and then the whole world — his schoolmates, the train station, everything he knew in downtown Hiroshima — was on fire. Closing his eyes was a hope that he was dreaming, that the bad thing coming at him was imagined, not real. So when the two masked men ran toward him, Mas closed his eyes.

When he opened them, the magic seemed to have worked, because he was still standing, albeit a little wobbly. The men were gone from his field of vision, but he could hear their footsteps behind him. Mas turned around and saw the men jump into a cable van (why had Mas missed that earlier?), rev the engine, and speed down the street.

Mas didn't waste any time trying to figure out why they had passed him by. He was used to being ignored, being passed over. An old Japanese man in sweaty, dirt-sodden clothes — he wouldn't take himself seriously either. Some would be angered by the slight, but Mas definitely saw his invisibility as an advantage, not a curse.

The woman's scream had come from inside the house, and Mas tried looking through the front picture window, but it was meticulously covered in newspaper from the inside like a paint-in-progress. He edged toward the screen door — the main door was still open. The hardwood floor was clear, aside from some balls of scrunched-up newspaper.

"Hallo," Mas called out. No response. He gingerly pulled open the screen and stepped into the house. Boxes lined the walls and most of the furniture was covered with white sheets. Not only did it seem like the neighbor was renovating, Mas also got the distinct feeling that she was on the move.

"Hallo," Mas said a little louder and then stayed quiet to hear a response. He thought that a muffled noise was emanating from a back room. He crept through the living room and poked his head into the next room, the kitchen. There on the floor was the old woman, who was covering her mouth with her hand, apparently trying to silence her cries. Two bags of groceries lay scattered beside her — obviously she had been frightened by the two men. Her beehive hairdo was now off-kilter and coming loose.

Mas crouched by a container of fresh orange juice turned on its side. "Youzu *orai,* lady?"

The woman shrieked again and pulled her legs back like a crab seeking refuge. One foot seemed bent awkwardly, as if she had hurt her ankle.

Mas looked around for the telephone and rose to pick up the receiver from the phone mounted on the wall.

"Who are you calling?" The woman suddenly got coherent.

"Police."

"No!" The woman hobbled herself up, clutching at the tile counter. "No police. They said no police."

He replaced the receiver on the hook and drew up a chair for the woman to rest her hurt foot. Somehow this act of kindness convinced the neighbor that she could trust

142

Mas, at least for a few more moments. She sat down and winced as she pulled up her injured foot. "I don't think it's broken," she said and Mas nodded. He had gotten into his share of scrapes on the job, and her pink ankle, at worst, might be slightly sprained. He went to the freezer and pulled out a bag of frozen corn. "Hold dis down," he ordered the woman, who eventually introduced herself as Sonya de Groot (no surprise to Mas). Mas didn't bother to introduce himself, so Sonya went ahead to connect the dots.

"You're a friend of Spoon, aren't you? You were the one at her house the other day."

Yah, you the one who called the police on me, Mas wanted to say, but he restrained himself. "My friend is Haruo, the guy Spoon was gonna marry."

"Yes, I heard that they canceled the wedding. Was that Haruo's doing or Spoon's?"

"Spoon."

"I see."

Mas didn't like the tone of that "I see." Mas was no wordsmith — far from it — because there was really no language that he completely called his own. But because he lacked a facility with words, he instead became an expert on inflections. He learned to read a person's frown lines in between the eyebrows, for example, the deliberate blinking of the eyes and the pursing of the lips. He listened for gaps in between words, how the voice went higher and lower or perhaps stayed completely flat. That "I see" meant that Sonya wasn't surprised, that she had a hunch that Spoon would break it off, stolen dolls or not.

"Itsu all about those Japanese *hina* dollsu."

Sonya's face turned ashen. "What about the dolls?"

"Somebody took them. Dat Dee say Haruo the one."

Sonya stopped icing her ankle and dropped the thawing bag of corn onto the linoleum floor. "When were they stolen?"

"Friday night."

"But then why —"

"Those guysu today, they want the dollsu?"

Sonya sucked her lips into her mouth and nodded.

"Youzu coulda just tole them to see Spoon."

Sonya shook her head. "I'd never do that. I'd never do anything that might put that woman in danger. She's like family. Our husbands were like brothers. Ike even lived with us before the accident, you know?"

Mas narrowed his eyes.

"Spoon didn't tell you or your friend, did she? They were on the brink of divorce. It was a big secret. I didn't understand. The hiding of their marital problems had to do with the Japanese culture — you know, shame and everything. They didn't even tell their daughters that they were living apart. The girls had moved out then, and well, Dee was having her own problems and living in that drug rehab facility. Whenever the family all came together, Ike would just move back home, like everything was normal hunky-dory."

Mas couldn't help but raise his eyebrows.

"I felt the same way. I would be worn out from all that deception, but I think Ike was really good at keeping secrets. Actually, my Jorg was good too, but maybe because he was so quiet. Never said a peep about anything. Ike, compared to Jorg, was the noisy one, actually, but he was on the quiet side as well. They were so similar inside but so different on the outside — Jorg must have been a foot taller and at least fifty pounds heavier. I joked that if it weren't for that and Ike being of Japanese ancestry and Jorg Dutch, they were identical twins."

Sonya laughed and Mas thought that he saw a moment of her youth in her smile. But as quickly as it descended on her face, the lightheartedness disappeared.

"We took care of Ike's family farm during the war, you know. Jorg even went up to that camp — Manzanar — up there in the Owens Valley to give regular reports. We helped the brothers some afterward too, when Ike spent a few years in Japan with the Occupation Forces."

Mas pretended he knew what Sonya was talking about, but it must have been pretty plain that he didn't.

"Your friend didn't know about that, huh? Ike kept it all hush-hush for some reason. Spoon lived there with him for a couple of years, I think."

Mas's jaw went slack. Spoon never let on that she had lived in Japan.

"Ike was also connected with that guayule project in Manzanar. You don't know about guayule, do you?"

"Izu ova in Japan during the war," Mas offered as an excuse.

"These flower growers and scientists from Caltech, they were trying to grow some natural rubber out there. Rubber was hard to come by during World War Two, so they started growing these guayule plants right in Manzanar to see if they could remedy the situation. Ike helped run the guayule farm in Manzanar. He thought that this guayule could be groundbreaking, help the United States be less dependent on foreign rubber, I guess. It all didn't work out. Jorg thinks that there might even have been some interference, you know, from tire manufacturers. They put guayule out of business, at least right after the war."

The more Mas learned of what these Nisei men and women did in camp, the more impressed he became. Yeah, second-generation Japanese Americans like Wishbone and Stinky weren't the epitome of respectability — they were definitely the bottom of the barrel, in fact — but even Mas had to give them credit for having some kick after being locked up by their own country. Like Haruo had bragged, this Ike was something else. He was an entrepreneur and he knew science. Just imagine what he would have done with his life if he hadn't been Japanese.

How could this man and his best friend, Jorg, have been dealing in drugs? It was *baka* talk, stupid and without reason. Casey had no clue. Casey had been angry and his anger had almost ensnared Mas, who wasn't going to dare breathe a word to Jorg's widow.

Mas knelt down to pick up the bag of frozen corn and had Sonya continue to cool her ankle. Luckily, it didn't seem serious, because the swelling was at a minimum.

"I don't know why everyone wants those dolls."

Mas readjusted his cap. "Eberyone?"

"My son, for example. When he heard about the dolls and that Spoon had purchased them, he was furious. Said some awful things, like Ike had led my husband astray . . . 'If it hadn't been for Ike, Dad would be with us now.' He wanted me to buy back the dolls. 'What were they doing in Dad's secret safe-deposit box?' he asked. I tried to get them, but Spoon was firm. She didn't want to let go of them and I can't blame her. I mean, they were from Ike's family, not ours. She got so upset with me and so did my son, Geoffrey. I was caught in the middle, and I didn't like it."

This story was slightly different from the one Spoon had shared with Mas. In Spoon's version, the de Groot woman had stopped talking to her for no reason. But here her lifetime friend and neighbor was also mourning the loss of their friendship.

"Didn't know Spoon even have money for dollsu," said Mas, not revealing how much was spent at Hina House.

"Well, she has her Dee account."

Mas raised his eyebrows.

"Ike's insurance money. From the very beginning she told me that she had it socked away in a special account for recovery programs for Dee. Rehab can be pretty expensive."

Mas nodded. Made sense that the mother would want to sacrifice comforts for her troubled daughter. He wondered how the two sisters felt about Dee's favored daughter status.

"I'm moving out of here now to live with Geoffrey and his family. Geoffrey insisted, especially after I started getting these calls about the dolls. Threatening calls, ugly calls. They didn't identify themselves and said they would divulge the truth about Jorg if I went to the police. I didn't know what they were talking about. Just scare tactics, I think. But when I told my son, he said that I should just keep it private, in the family. He told me then that I should move to his house in Oceanside."

Sonya pushed back a wayward hair that had gotten loose from the tumbleweed on her head. "My grandchildren are still at the age where they don't mind being with their grammy, so I'm going along with the move. But I like being on my own, so this will be a hard adjustment."

Mas explained that he was in the same

boat as Sonya. "I gotsu a new roommate too. Haruo."

"Friends living together can really test the relationship." Sonya nodded. "Some of us are just meant to live alone."

The phone began ringing and the old woman jumped as if it were the sound of gunshot.

Like Mas, she didn't have an answering machine, so the phone kept ringing and ringing.

"They'll keep calling until someone picks up."

Mas figured he would do the honors and lifted the receiver. He had barely put it to his ear when a male voice declared, "Bitch, just give us what your husband left or we won't leave you alive next time."

Mas slammed down the phone without saying anything.

"He said something horrible, didn't he?"

"Youzu betta go ova to your kid's house. Sooner than later."

"I certainly don't want to stay here alone tonight. But I'm too tired to drive."

Mas scratched his head. Oceanside was at least a good two- to three-hour drive away during rush hour. Although he wanted to help, his help had limits — not beyond one hour's worth.

"I could take the train and have my son fetch the car later. He comes once a week to the market, anyway," she proposed.

"Izu take you ova to Union Station."

Sonya met Mas's eyes and she nodded. She limped to her bedroom where a suitcase was already opened and half filled.

Before they left the bare ranch-style house, Sonya looked around wistfully. "A lot of memories here," she murmured. "Memories of Jorg too."

Her rumination reminded Mas of what his customers and Nisei women had told him after Chizuko's funeral: "You'll always carry her memory in your heart" and "She'll always be with you."

But the truth was, as time passed, a little of Chizuko faded with it. If Mas ever moved out of that McNally Street house, his once intact family — as small as it was — might be forever obliterated. So he hung on to the past, at least the second-chance past in America. It hadn't been all happy, but at least it was familiar.

It took Mas only about half an hour to drive the widow to downtown L.A. Traditional rush hour had officially ended, but these days, with all the downtown lofts and sports stadiums, the freeways could be jammed when you least expected it.

151

"Oh, we're here already." The widow was also surprised when Mas stopped the Ford in front of a prettified Union Station. It always had been impressive, with its high ceilings, cool Spanish tile floor, and curved archways, but there had been a time where the historic building had become dingy, almost obsolete. But now with light rail and subway tracks crisscrossing the county, the train station was recently more in vogue.

He jumped out to help the hobbling Sonya, but by the time he reached the other side, she was ready to go with her suitcase.

"You're very worried about your friend, aren't you?"

Mas nodded.

"You don't think that he took the dolls."

No. Mas spoke through his eyes, his pupils dark and solid in the diffused light emanating from the corner of the Art Deco building.

"There's someone who might be able to help you," Sonya said. "Actually, someone who I've known for a very long time. He was the police detective who had been assigned to Jorg and Ike's accident. Chuck Blanco. He doesn't work for the police anymore. He's an inspector on his own. But he still is keenly interested in what happened to Jorg.

"You see, he doesn't think that it was an accident. He never did. I think that he might have even lost his job over Jorg and Ike's case."

Mas felt as if freezing cold water was being poured over his head.

"Anyway, about a year ago, I began receiving these strange postcards. Typewritten. All gibberish. I reported them to my local postal inspector, but there was little he could do. They weren't threatening. They just didn't make any sense. The same thing over and over again. Without a return address but a Phoenix postmark.

"So I called Mr. Blanco. Not that he could do anything, but I thought that he'd be interested. And he was. So I mailed some of the postcards to him. Shortly thereafter, the postcards stopped coming. But Mr. Blanco told me to inform him if anything unusual came up again."

"You tellsu him about dollsu?"

The widow nodded her head. "Of course, first thing. Like I said, Mr. Blanco is very committed to finding out the truth about the car accident. Spoon never cared for him, however. She won't talk to him. So I'd appreciate it if you don't mention it to her that I still keep in touch with him."

Mas bit down on the right side of his lip.

153

Too many secrets between supposed friends.

A train must have just released carloads of commuters because they spilled out of the station, their briefcases swollen with tasks undone.

"Find out who was sendin' the cards?" Mas finally asked.

"Never did. I almost completely forgot about those postcards, in fact. Then I came across one this week when I was packing. But only this time I understood the word that was typed." The widow rummaged through her purse and presented a bent postcard to Mas. In the darkness and without his glasses, Mas couldn't make out the words, only that they were typewritten.

Sonya stepped in to interpret. " 'HINA,' it says. 'HINA,' almost twenty times over."

Hina. Had it been some strange coincidence? Why had someone written a word referring to the Girls' Day dolls? And a year ago, much less? Mas was troubled and a bit spooked, in fact. Dolls sometimes seemed to be inhabited by spirits — such as those at Hina House in San Diego. Had Ike's *hina* dolls somehow inspired a message? No, that was too ridiculous to consider.

There must be something *tokubetsu* about those dolls. Not historic or cultural, but perhaps more specific. Did they serve as a hiding place? And if so, for what?

Driving home, Mas knew that to piece together this puzzle, he'd have to sit down and make peace with Haruo. They said two heads — even considering Haruo's lackluster one — were better than one.

As soon as Mas turned onto McNally and then into his driveway, he noticed something familiar from Mari's childhood days. The door, and in fact the screen door too, was *akkepanashi,* wide open, inviting any wandering flies or robbers to enter. "Sonafugun," Mas murmured. Recollections of all of Haruo's annoying traits, as bad as a teenager's, washed over him again.

Carrying the six-pack of room-temperature Coke and the can of cashews, Mas slammed the driver's door. "Haruo!" he called out, walking onto the front porch. The stink of something burning filled his nostrils and a film of smoke obscured his vision.

"Haruo!" Mas bellowed again, but nothing. He went straight into the kitchen, where the smoke was thickest, and heard water rushing from the faucet. A figure standing at the sink turned. The Buckwheat Beauty, holding a pan, charred and damaged beyond repair.

■ ■ ■ ■

To find his best friend's nemesis in the middle of his faded kitchen was a shock indeed. "Whatchu doin' here?"

"Uh, saving your ass and your house from going up in flames. Don't you know better than to leave the house while dinner's on the stove?" Dee shot back without hesitation.

Mas went to the sink and turned off the faucet. What nerve this woman had to be in another's man's house! "Not cookin' nuttin'. You the one makin' dis mess." *And I expect you to clean it too,* Mas added silently.

"Look, I came here to talk to Haruo. When I got here, the front door was wide open and smoke was blowing out onto the street. Nobody was home."

"Sonafugun," Mas muttered. A couple of sliced rounds of carrots were left on the white plastic cutting board and a crushed cardboard package for curry blocks had been tossed in the trash can. Haruo, no doubt, had started to make dinner. But why would he leave without finishing what he started? Before he could figure out what happened to Haruo, Mas needed to clear his head of Spoon's daughter. "*Orai,* so

youzu save the day. Good for you. Haruo
not here, go talk to him tomorrow at market."

"I will. But I wanted to see him sooner. I
think that my mother may be having a
nervous breakdown."

Mas bit down on his lip. Spoon was on
his blacklist, but not enough for him to wish
her an emotional meltdown.

"She won't leave the bedroom and won't
let anyone in. Doesn't want to see any of
us girls. She even threw me out of the
house."

Mas raised his eyebrow. *Sō-ka,* he thought.
*Seems like every homeless person ends up
in my house.* Good thing he had stopped by
the market for a full baker's dozen of ramen
packages.

"She won't see a therapist. I thought
maybe Haruo could talk to her. She still
cares about him, you know."

*You wouldn't know that judging from her
recent actions,* Mas thought.

"My mother is hiding something. I think
it has to do with those dolls. I know, I
thought Haruo had stolen them. But now I
don't know."

Dee's doubts about her previous suspicion
did little to cool Mas's anger. She was the
one who had sent the law after Haruo in

the first place. He marched out of the kitchen and returned to the front door. He checked the screen. It wasn't just open; someone had given it a big tug so that it was almost unhinged from the frame. The screen had been broken before, but Mas had made the time to repair it last year. Outside on the concrete porch were skid marks from the heels of someone's shoes.

"Youzu do dis to my house?"

Dee shook her head. "I just went straight in. I didn't even touch the screen door."

Mas traced physical clues, a spray of gravel, a trail of open cement where a blanket of dried sycamore leaves had been. He took a big sniff. A familiar, delectable smell, one that made his mouth water. On the side of the cracked driveway, by some pigweed threatening to overtake the neighbor's lawn, lay a spoon covered in fresh curry. And tangled in the leaves of a knee-high weed, long, greasy black-and-white hairs pulled out from their roots, their ends stained with blood.

Mas knew what the theories at the Eaton Nursery would be — that Haruo had perhaps faked his disappearance because he had actually stolen the dolls to pay off bookies and loan sharks. But they hadn't seen the masked men at Sonya de Groot's house.

158

Or listened to the talk about cocaine at the market.

"Haruo's in trouble," Mas murmured to himself and then louder for his one witness's benefit, "big trouble."

CHAPTER EIGHT

Making other people believe that Haruo was in big trouble was a larger challenge than Mas bargained for. The Buckwheat Beauty wouldn't leave Mas's house, but he wouldn't let her stop what had to be done. First was a call to G.I. Hasuike and Juanita Gushiken, the closest thing to a crime-fighting duo that he knew of. But G.I. and Juanita, busy with their lawyering and private investigating, respectively, were unmoved.

"I mean, why would anyone want to kidnap Haruo?" asked G.I. over the phone.

A very good question, Mas thought, a good question that he didn't have an answer for. Haruo had no money, no house, and no working car. His children, both teachers, weren't rich. His ex-wife had indeed remarried, but to a television repairman who had retired his shingle as soon as people were paying companies to take old broken television sets off their hands.

"And those men who were at Spoon's neighbor's house — are you sure that they weren't just kids causing trouble?" asked Juanita on the other line.

No, no, no, Mas tried to tell them. In spite of the ski masks, he knew the difference between a wild gangly teenager's build and a grown man's. Plus they had threatened Sonya, not only in person but also in telephone calls — but he had promised the old lady that he wouldn't breathe a word about that.

"Well, you can file a report with the sheriff's department. When they find out about Haruo's background . . . I just don't know, Mas. If that neighbor woman goes to the police about her two intruders, it might be a different story."

Next on Mas's list was Kimiyi, Haruo's daughter, who also didn't seem to understand the gravity of what was being told to her. "Missing?"

"*Ka-re* burnin' right on the stove."

"Oh."

Why, just *oh?* thought Mas, his temper rising.

"Did he ever tell you how he left the house while he was filling up the bathtub when we were children? Our hardwood floors got all warped."

This has nothing to do with an overflowing bathtub, Mas wanted to yell. A chunk of Haruo's hair had been left in the driveway. What else was being done to him right this moment?

The daughter was so passive, Mas had to move on to the son. He knew from the get-go that Clement would not be happy to hear from Mas, much less about his estranged father.

"Are you sure he's not back at it?"

Mas bit down on his dentures. It had indeed been a mistake to call the son, but he didn't know what else to do.

"You know what I'm talking about. Did you check the card clubs in Gardena, the Indian casinos in Temecula? Las Vegas, even?"

Mas had no answer.

Apparently the son distinctly remembered pulling his father back from those tables, time after time. "When you search all those places and you still can't find him, I'll know something's wrong. But until then, don't bother calling back."

"No luck?" said Dee, bringing a cup of freshly brewed Yuban coffee to Mas at the kitchen table. Mas was going to refuse it, but what was the use? The Buckwheat

Beauty was not stupid. Even overhearing only Mas's clipped side of the conversation, she knew that no one took his concerns seriously. Mas understood the bitterness of children. He himself had been an absent father and had experienced the fallout from neglect. He was trying to mend fences now, two thousand miles away, and it was like tending a sick orchid — no flowers, but the bare stem of hope was still standing.

Mas took a sip of the coffee, so hot that it burned his tongue. He didn't mind because the pain jump-started his brain. It was already close to eleven and no Haruo. Wishbone and Stinky hadn't seen him. Neither had his boss, Taxie. Other than receiving a phone call about the wedding cancellation, Tug hadn't spoken to Haruo in a few weeks.

"I think we'd better call the sheriff."

Mas looked up, surprised. Not because the Buckwheat Beauty was suggesting that they contact the authorities, but because she had said "we."

The first thing Mas did when the sheriff's deputies stepped into the house was hand over the plastic bag with the bloody strands of hair. Mas had seen enough television crime dramas to know that hair could unravel secrets of the most pernicious and hidden crimes. The Altadena law enforcement officers, however, seemed more skeptical. Dressed in brown uniforms, they were congenial enough, patiently spelling out Haruo's first name a couple of times before they got it right.

"Now, would there be any reason why Mr. Mukai would want to run away from his life?" one of the deputies asked.

Mas mumbled unintelligibly and the Buckwheat Beauty looked down at her high-top tennis shoes.

"You know, woman problems, maybe any trouble with the police?"

Yes and yes would have been the correct answers, but Mas and Dee shook their heads.

"Do you have a photo?" they asked.

Mas sat frozen in his living room chair, thinking desperately of where he might have an image of Haruo other than the one in his head.

"I do," said the Buckwheat Beauty, surprisingly. She brought out keys to the delivery truck, which were attached to a wallet. Inside the wallet were a few plastic compartments for photos. One was of Dee, her two sisters, and their parents when Ike was alive. The other was a more recent group shot of the family, including Haruo in the back.

One of the deputies brought the photo close to his face. "You weren't exaggerating about the scar," he said to Mas. "It is pretty severe. How did he get it?"

Mas knew that Haruo had many different versions of the birth of his scar. House fire. Spousal abuse. Anthing except the truth — the Bomb — because it just caused too much discomfort for the inquirer. It turned out that Mas didn't have to manufacture anything because the Buckwheat Beauty beat him to it.

"Kitchen fire, when he was a kid in Japan," said Dee. Her answer surprised Mas, not because it was a lie, but because she said it so easily, flippantly, as if she really believed it. Mas crossed his arms, jamming his fists into his armpits. Wait a minute. She really did believe it. Why hadn't Haruo told her the truth?

There were doubles of the same photo in the sleeve of the wallet, so Dee gave the less worn one to the deputies.

"We'll send out his name with the photo. If anyone finds a person matching his description, they'll let us know."

Mas felt his dentures click together. He knew what the deputy was saying. If they found an unidentified dead body in a hospital or in a ditch, Haruo Mukai would be on the list of possible John Does. What good was that, identifying Haruo when he was dead when they needed to find him while alive?

Still, Mas got up from his easy chair and bowed his head in thanks.

"Maybe he'll show up at work," Dee said, a little too brightly, after the deputies had left the house. They had told them not to worry, to rest, but that's the last thing Mas could do.

He wondered if Dee was going to tell her mother what was going on. If Spoon was indeed having a nervous breakdown, maybe news of Haruo's disappearance would be too much. Either way, he'd let the daughter take care of dispatching the news to the Hayakawa side. He had already been a target of Spoon's reactionary mood swings and wanted to stand clear of any more.

He went into the kitchen to pour himself another cup of coffee. It was lukewarm by now, but Mas didn't care.

The two of them sat at the kitchen table and stayed quiet for a while. In fact, the whole house was so still that Mas could hear the ticking from his bowling trophy clock in his bedroom.

"You know, we used to have a kitchen set like this." Dee spread her arms over the table surface, which was tattooed with soy sauce stains and cigarette burns. "Formica, right? That's what they call it?"

Formica, whatever, what did that have to do with anything? Mas wondered.

Dee tipped her head back, and again, for a flash, Mas could see a glimpse of her former beauty. "I was sitting with my dad like this on the morning he died. He was up at three, like always, and I hadn't even slept yet. I watched him do his little routine, you know, boil an egg for six minutes, let it cool, and then crack it open about fifteen minutes later. Then he'd spread a thick layer of Best Foods mayonnaise over the top and sprinkle some black pepper over that. He did that every morning. Mom said she'd boil the eggs for him beforehand, but he said he didn't like how the yolk would get dark on the outside. Dad was kind of like that egg. All perfect. No marks. When I started getting into trouble, I thought for sure he'd lose it. Yell, hit me. In rehab, you know, my parents had to come in for our family sessions. I had to get into it. Everything I did. Where I bought drugs. When I was arrested. The whole time my mom would be holding her purse, ready to make her getaway at any minute, while Dad had his head down, like what I did was his fault.

"Anyway, that day he got killed, he must have known that something bad was going to happen. Because after he ate his egg, he looked at me. Right at me. 'Take care of your mother,' he said. 'Whatever you do, take care of her.'

"I knew that I needed to stop him, tell him not to go to Hanley. But I didn't follow through. And that's something I've regretted every day since. So if you think Haruo's in trouble, you can't just give up and let the police handle it. Because they don't know Haruo like you do."

Mas looked at his Casio watch. Haruo was missing now for seven hours. A lot could happen in seven hours. In fact, in a few seconds the day could become night and the skies could bleed black. Both Mas and Haruo had witnessed it for themselves. The Buckwheat Beauty was right: Time was not often on Mas's side and, for that matter, not on Haruo's, either.

Mas fell asleep right at the kitchen table and woke when he heard the *thump-thump* of newspapers being delivered to some of his neighbors' homes. The Buckwheat Beauty was gone, probably off to work at the market. Before Mas could figure out what to do next, the phone rang.

He answered it on the second ring. "Hallo," he said, louder than any man should at five o'clock in the morning.

"Mas, it's Taxie. Sorry to call so early, but you told me to call you if Haruo showed up, right?"

Mas swallowed. His throat felt scratchy and parched.

"Yeah, well, he didn't come in. I'm kind of worried because he hasn't missed a day of work since he started." Taxie must have been on a cell phone because the reception was poor, causing crackling and popping in between every word.

"And, well, I hate to tell you this, Mas, but I thought you should know — he's been going to the track a couple times a week for the past three months. Sometimes with Casey. Casey didn't want anyone to know, but the parking attendant noticed them leaving together and Haruo let it slip one day that they were going to Santa Anita. I just found out myself this morning."

Mas's stomach fell. Haruo was back gambling? In a way, it should not have been a surprise. Mas had heard Americans saying that someone's eyes were too big for his stomach. Well, Haruo's eyes were much too big for his wallet. Being the optimist that he was, he always thought that the pot of gold or happy ending awaited him *if.* If he stayed at the poker table for one more round. If he tossed the dice one more time. That kind of hope could lead to only one thing — death. Either a physical death at the hands of a loan shark's dispatcher or a death of a spiritual kind. Haruo had been resurrected from the latter, but Mas doubted that his friend or even he could survive another incident.

While speaking to Taxie, Mas silently cursed Haruo, Casey, and the gambling sickness. "Youzu see Casey at the market?"

More crackling.

"You know, I actually haven't seen him this morning. But then he doesn't come in every day."

"Where he live?"

"He's between places. I think he's living in an apartment next to the Japanese Episcopal Church right now. The one in Koreatown."

Mas could hear potential flower customers in the background inquiring about the cost of different blooms, so he let Taxie return to business.

If Casey had been the one to lead Haruo astray, church or no church, there would be hell to pay.

The Japanese Episcopal Church in Los Angeles was smack-dab in the middle of Koreatown. The area had been referred to as Uptown before the war, and Japanese immigrants, mostly gardeners, once lived in bungalows north and south of there.

Mas knew where the church was, but he had never gone inside. Mari had gone — or, rather, was sent to — Japanese school every Saturday morning a few blocks away. Mas and Chizuko actually didn't know how many times Mari actually graced the doors of her classroom because they had heard about and even seen her loitering outside with another girl smoking cigarettes. It seemed that the more Chizuko pushed Mari to be Japanese, the more she declared herself to be American. Mas was actually sympathetic, because he often felt the same way, only that he couldn't properly speak either Japanese or English, making him without not only a language but also a country.

The church was once flanked by a Korean-owned golf driving range, green netting as tall as the neighboring mini-high-rises. Now the golf range had been replaced by a new elementary school with an impressive multicolored pagoda on one side. The voices of children playing during recess somehow lifted Mas's spirits.

He parked on the street and as he neared the modest chapel he spied a couple of neon yellow golf balls in the driveway. He picked them up — he didn't know why, but they seemed to be crying out to be claimed.

The apartment, the orange color of Ritz crackers, stood above a vegetable garden surrounded by a locked gate. Judging from the look of the soil and its maintenance, the garden was relatively new. There were beds of carrots, melons, beets, and radishes. In between potted lemon trees, another golf ball, looking like a recently laid white egg, had fallen.

Mas walked around the imprisoned garden to gain access to the apartment building. A row of battered metal mailboxes in front of a staircase held few clues. There were numbers but no names. Would Mas have to knock on each door to find where Casey lived?

As he mulled over his options, a mustached man carrying a golf club appeared from the staircase. "You have my balls."

"Excuse?"

"Golf balls." The man gestured toward the neon yellow dimpled balls held in Mas's right hand.

"Oh, yah." Somewhat embarrassed, Mas forfeited the balls. He was just trying to be a good samaritan, not a bloody *dorobō*.

"You lookin' for somebody?" The urban golfer eyed him suspiciously.

"Casey Nakayama."

"Mista Casey?"

Casey would be the last person Mas thought of as a "Mister" with a capital *M,* but he wasn't going to publicly dispute it.

"He outta town, I think. Go ova to church. They may know."

It was still early, so Mas didn't expect to find many people at the church. But there was a steady flow of mothers walking their knee-high children into one of the buildings.

"You want to go to the chapel?" a woman who acted like a teacher asked him. She stood in a room surrounded by toys and tables.

Mas nodded. The woman directed him through the classroom down a hall. The doors of the church were open but the lights were dim. A *hakujin* woman with frizzy graying hair was stacking some kind of book on the back table.

"I lookin' for man in charge," Mas said.

"I'm the rector, so I guess it would be me."

Mas felt his cheeks flush. He wasn't a church man, either regular or even sporadic, unless you counted funerals. He didn't realize that head pastors of a Japanese church could be a *hakujin,* much less a woman.

"I lookin' for Casey Nakayama."

"Casey told us yesterday that he was going up north to see his brother for a while. His brother's been sick with cancer. I don't think that he has much more time. Can I help you with anything?"

Mas shook his head and his eyes caught glimpses of color above. He had seen stained-glass windows before, but nothing like these. There were at least a dozen long windows facing each other. Instead of looking reverent and austere, they seemed happy and schizophrenic — privy to private jokes and secrets unknown to the public.

For instance, there was the mother with her child Jesus, but down below on the same pane was the dog in the *Peanuts* cartoon — Snoopy, isn't that what Mari had called her stuffed animal? And then on another pane, all ten detention camps where the Nisei like Tug, Wishbone and Stinky, Spoon and Ike had been locked up. And on another one, fish and flowers alongside a push mower.

"I heard about dis," Mas said.

"Yes, that one represents all the occupations of our early parishioners. Fishermen, produce workers, flower growers, gardeners. They call them Issei, first-generation Japanese, right?"

Mas nodded.

"We just started that garden outside in the memory of our founding minister. Casey helped out from time to time, but mostly people from our Spanish-language congregation are tending it."

"Nice, nice," Mas murmured. He thanked the rector and headed back to the truck. This stop in Koreatown had been a waste. Mas didn't know if Casey had been feeding the rector a line about being a dutiful brother. Casey didn't seem the type to sit attentively beside a dying person, but you never know how people react at times of death. Some people cry with all their might, their heads back like a wolf howling at the moon. Others run around in circles. Quite a few take off as fast as they can, a rocket shooting out from the mess of the earth. Mas had been that way when Chizuko was dying — maybe not physically but emotionally — and his escape strategy had never fully been forgiven by his daughter.

The Episcopal church held no clues, so now Mas was off to the churches of the faithful gambler. To Santa Anita racetrack.

Hollywood Park. Hustler Casino and Normandie Club in Gardena. Bicycle Casino in Bell Gardens. And all the assorted gambling joints in lower Los Angeles.

By the time Mas got home, his body felt literally broken. Not in two, but pulverized in fractured pieces. Over the course of the day, he saw many men who looked like Haruo — short, shrunken Asian men with oily hair and baseball caps. One even sported a gash on his cheek. But none of them was Haruo.

Mas spent most of the evening staring at one of the many cobwebs growing in the corners of his house. He remembered how Haruo had been the one who visited Mas every single damn day when Chizuko was hospitalized and the subsequent months after she died. Haruo would sit on the couch — the same one on which he had recently slept — and revel in minutiae about his day and the day of other friends and even strangers. He'd go on like this for hours. Even when Mas finally dragged himself from his easy chair, turned off the television set, and lay down on his mattress in the bedroom, he could hear Haruo prattle on and on. A part of Mas wanted to throw Haruo out of the house on his ear, but the truth was, the mindless talking served as

Mas's lullaby, causing him to finally fall asleep.

At about ten o'clock, later than any human should be calling another, the phone rang. "Mas, I've got some bad news." It was Taxie and Mas feared the worst. He pictured Haruo's mangled body, crushed by a car. But instead, Taxie mentioned another name. "Casey Nakayama. He was found shot dead in an alley outside of the market."

CHAPTER NINE

No one knew how long the corpse had been there. Casey's dead body had been discovered by a homeless man in search of discarded plastic bottles and aluminum cans in the nearby Dumpster. "We saw him last on Wednesday," said Taxie. Wednesday was the same day Haruo went missing.

"Heezu has a brotha up north," Mas murmured. Isn't that what the church lady had told him?

"Casey? He's the only boy of all sisters. He doesn't have any brothers."

The next morning, Mas went to the flower market first thing. Crime-scene tape blocked the alley, and pockets of men stood outside leering, as if Casey's ghost would suddenly make an appearance. There were even a couple of homeless men, one a seven-foot black man with a large head that drooped down like the shell of a bean sprout.

Although it was the same windowless

concrete building, the lively insides had been sucked dry with news of Casey's death. Workers and regular customers were in a state of disbelief. "Did you hear about Casey?" "Can you believe what happened to Casey?" was the background music for the entire day.

Mas found Pico sleepwalking through his duties, moving a box of baskets from one side of storage to another. He was relieved to see Mas, who understood the inner workings and even secrets of the market yet was an outsider.

"He was sitting right here a couple of days ago. I still halfway think that this is one of his put-ons, you know. Like any minute, he'll be walking in the market, saying, 'Gotcha, gotcha,' and laughing. But he's not coming back, is he?" Pico waited to see Mas nod, anything that would make reality stick.

"Somebody take his money?"

"The police don't think that it was robbery. He was shot through the head, execution style." Sounded like a page out of a gangster novel. Casey wasn't an angel, but he wasn't completely on the dark side, either.

"He tellsu some folks dat he goin' away."

"Yeah, that's what he told me. That he was going up to Laughlin for a few weeks.

Struck me as kinda strange because Casey didn't really go anywhere far."

"So heezu seems just the same, no different?"

"You know, on Wednesday, while we were playing liar's poker, he got this phone call. His face just went white, and I don't mean *hakujin* white, but ghost white." It was strange for a *hakujin* like Pico to use that term, but Mas figured that he had spent too much time with Japanese. "I don't know who was on the other line, but Casey wasn't happy to hear from him. He first says, 'How'd you get this number?' And then he listens and says, 'Okay, okay.' Sounded to me like he was going to meet up with someone later that day. But he didn't say anything to us."

"Heezu always seems to have sumptin' up his sleeve."

"Well, yeah, he was involved in a couple of schemes. Chump change, if you ask me. He was taking a lot of homeless guys to the track. Wasn't sure what that was all about. And one time this guy in a suit comes in, panting almost like a dog, crying that he got found out by his wife about something he did, so he needs to be extra, extra careful. Sounded like he was having an affair and Casey was somehow involved. Didn't

180

ask, didn't want to know."

The light in the storage area was so dim that it washed all color from Pico's face and clothes.

"Wheresu dat Roberto guy, anyhow?"

"That's the thing. He calls in his resignation yesterday. Said that he had to go to be with his sick mother in El Salvador."

Mas grunted. Casey's supposed cancer-ridden brother in Northern California, Roberto's mother in Central America — fake and supposedly real relatives in the market seemed to be dropping like flies.

After visiting the flower market, Mas went up to the maze of Silver Lake to Juanita Gushiken's small house in back of her parents'. She lived part time in G.I.'s house but never gave up her primary residence. "Don't want to disappear in G.I.'s world," she had told Mas, who didn't quite understand.

He had called beforehand, just to make sure that she would be at home. First thing she said when she opened the door was, "Sorry that we weren't able to do much when you called about Haruo being missing."

Mas understood. Young people — even middle-aged people — had their own lives,

181

and it should be that way. He had no expectation that his own daughter Mari should dote on him, although his late wife Chizuko might have.

"You have that postcard?" Juanita asked, referring to the one with the cryptic "HINA" message that Sonya had received.

"I gotsu it in the car."

Mas retrieved it from the glove compartment — only a few dirt smudges, which he attempted to remove but managed to create more of a mess.

Juanita examined the photo side, four different views of Phoenix: a large red rock formation, a cavemanlike drawing, a totem pole in front of a museum, and a cow town. "Doesn't look like a regular postcard. It's like those free corporate kinds from hotel chains. I have a friend who works at a resort in Phoenix; I'll scan this and e-mail it to her."

Mas told the private investigator about Casey's body in the alley.

"What the hell? I was just over there a month ago picking up some leis for my girlfriend's birthday party. It's a pretty sketchy area, but still, a murder? Do you think that this guy's death has anything to do with Haruo's disappearance?"

"I dunno. Three guys gone missing from

there in two days."

"And you think that it goes back to this postcard and maybe those dolls?"

Mas couldn't explain why he thought Haruo's disappearance had something to do with Spoon and her late husband, only that he smelled a connection. Juanita promised to make the identification of the postcard and its anonymous sender her first priority.

Once Mas was safely at home, he should have had some sense of *ochitsuki*. *Ochitsuki* literally meant falling into stickiness, to have presence of mind or be calm. He had done what he could, right? He had informed the sheriff in Altadena of Haruo's disappearance, approached the daughter Kiyomi and the son Clement, and elicited Juanita's help. But Mas's mind wandered to a place where two other men lost their lives twenty years ago. He dug out some old AAA maps for California and found the small town of Hanley, barely a pinprick underneath the larger circle for the city of Brawley. As Chizuko always did, he took out a yellow highlighter (his were all dried out, however) and attempted to draw the route from Pasadena through Palm Springs and then to Imperial Valley.

He had tossed most of his dead highlighters and had moved on to a red pen when someone knocked on his door. He wasn't surprised to see the Buckwheat Beauty on the other side of the busted screen door.

"No word on Haruo?"

Mas shook his head, the map still bunched up in his fist.

"Are you planning to go somewhere?" she asked, and then her eyes widened when she recognized Mas's red pen path to Imperial Valley. She moved the screen door over so she could enter the house.

"Why are you going there, of all places?" she asked.

Mas described his conversation with Sonya de Groot and her suggestion that the former detective Blanco might have some answers. Dee apparently didn't think the same way.

"The guy's an asshole. And he's a terrible detective. He has all these pet theories that he just makes up in his mind — too much TV, if you ask me. He even tried to say that my father's accident was my fault, that I had scored some drugs from the wrong people in town. Then it turns out that his boss finds a brick of cocaine in his car. He tries to pin that on me too. Says it's my people who did that to him."

Mas must have plainly worn his skepticism on his face because Dee spat out, "Hey, I admit that I've made some mistakes. But I didn't cause my father's death, all right? I've been clean. This time for seven months now."

The Buckwheat Beauty said seven months as if it were seven decades. *You triple or quadruple that,* Mas thought, *and then I'll think it's a big deal.*

Dee took a couple of short breaths as she listened to Mas explain the repetitive message on the postcards Sonya had received. "Sounds like they were sent from some kind of wacko. Plus Auntie Sonya says the postcards stopped last year, right? What would that have to do with the dolls?"

After going back and forth with Mas like in a Ping-Pong match, Dee finally conceded. "If you insist on going, then I'll go with you. But you'll have to drive. I'm not going to waste any gas to go to Hanley."

Some people looked for signs to know where they were going, but Mas relied on landmarks. For Dr. Svelick's, it was the community garden on the corner; for his Wednesday customer, it was the San Gabriel Mission. For Imperial Valley, the landmarks didn't appear every couple of miles but every seventy-five. They were notable ones — larger-than-life markers seen even in the deadness of early dawn. The sloping backs of the dinosaur statues, as big as bank buildings, along I-10 at Cabazon, not far from some shopping outlets. The crop of windmills, their blades as ominous as kamikaze plane propellers, outside of Palm Springs. And before Mas knew it, the Ford was firmly in the grip of the desert — not the shiny version with pristine pools populated by skin-damaged *hakujin* old women in leopard-patterned swimsuits, but the true desert, the brown barrenness that sucked moisture from a man's lips and cheeks and insides. It was certainly a sign that this place was not for human habitation. Only the ugliest and thorniest plants and creatures seemed naturally up to the task.

Yet, people persevered. In places like Cathedral City, a retirement town, where most of the front yards were multicolored crushed bits of granite. Or Indio, marked by palm trees diapered below their feathered fronds to catch ripened dates.

South of those signs of life came the Salton Sea, invisible from I-86. It was just as well because Mas remembered it as being a leaky sink filled with dirty dishwater. The outline of the television satellite dishes and shoe box–shaped trailers dotting the land-scape made Mas feel especially lonely. The Buckwheat Beauty had fallen asleep by now (so much for her offer to drive once they reached Palm Springs), so Mas shivered in the Ford alone.

Once they passed the southern tip of Salton Sea, Mas shook off the bleakness and his memory kicked in. He remembered the rows of cantaloupe and honeydew melons swollen in the fields after World War Two. He dealt more with tomatoes and did his share of picking on a Nisei farm on the north side, in a town called Niland. Every time they dug down, they hit rock, quite literally. When hoes or shovels couldn't do it, the farmers had to bring out the big guns — tractors with forklift teeth — to remove the giant stones. Soon, a stacked pile of rocks would be on the edge of the fields, ready for the taking.

By the time they were on the outskirts of Brawley, the sun was starting to make an appearance. Dee stirred, squinted, and then rubbed her eyes with the tops of her fists like a child.

"I need coffee," she said and Mas agreed. He stopped at a gas station mini-mart.

"Where the hell are we?" Dee asked. They sat at a plastic table outside covered in graffiti in some unrecognizable language. All Mas could make out was the number 13 splattered in permanent ink.

The coffee in their Stryofoam cups looked bad and tasted worse. Mas was just thankful for anything to help recharge his batteries. As always, he drank his coffee black, while Dee opened two packages of sugar and a package of fake powdered cream in a triple tear and dumped it on the surface of the brackish-looking liquid. One stir with her index finger and then she winced after drinking.

"Weezu a coupla miles north of Brawley," Mas said.

The Buckwheat Beauty's face fell and Mas figured that it must still be fatigue. "Need to get something."

Mas held his cup with both hands and looked out at the skyline. In spite of the hollow outline of the sun, grayness prevailed. Low-lying shrubs pinched at any moisture they could find in the flat brown ground. It was still fairly cool, but Mas could feel some oppressive heat gather above their heads.

Dee came out with two red pens with artificial nylon roses sticking out from one end.

"I gotsu pens," Mas said, referring to his

assorted collection in the old L.A. Clippers basketball mug glued to his dashboard. But the girl ignored him.

They both tossed their half-drunk coffee in the wire trash can by the mini-mart door and got back into the Ford. They had traveled only a mile when the Buckwheat Beauty started waving her hands.

"Stop!" she cried and Mas pumped down on the brakes. The Ford jackknifed slightly as he eased it to the side of the highway.

The Buckwheat Beauty jumped out of the truck before Mas could ask why. She ran across the two-lane highway and laid the flower pens on the road like a religious offering and seemed to be mouthing some sort of prayer. Mas realized that it was here where her father and Ike had died. For her sake and maybe her father's, Mas lowered his eyes as well. As she ran back to the car, Mas noticed the wind carry the rose pens out to the highway. They kept rolling and rolling until a RV going north ran over them, squashing the pens with its giant wheels and releasing the fabric petals, which flapped for a moment like the severed wings of a butterfly before being buried in dust.

When they reached Hanley, the Buckwheat Beauty guided Mas to the downtown business district, where she instructed him to park in front of a set of buildings hidden behind a Spanish-style façade.

She pointed to the second-floor window where Blanco's office was supposed to be located. "He's not any kind of real inspector now, you know. Used to work for the Department of Agriculture and then started his own business inspecting organics. I don't know why he's still hung up on my dad's accident. I guess he thinks it ended his law enforcement career."

Mas took a couple of gulps of air. He didn't relish facing Blanco on his own, but it was clear that the Buckwheat Beauty's presence would lead to more harm than good.

He pulled on the tarnished metal handle of the glass door. Inside, he noted the building directory — little plastic white letters pushed onto a black board. C. BLANCO, INSPECTOR, ROOM 206. He made his way up the dusty stairs and finally identified the right room. The numbers, each digit a sticker, were curled up from age and hard to read.

Mas rapped on the door with his knuckles. "Come in."

Sitting at an old oak desk was a chubby middle-aged man with a bald head and heavy sideburns shaped like two states of California. He immediately smiled when he saw Mas.

"Hashimoto? Onion man, right?"

Mas took off his Dodger cap and shook his head. "Mas. Mas Arai."

Blanco frowned and flipped through his datebook. "I don't have any Arai down. When did you call?"

"Didn't callsu. Izu here wiz Dee Hayakawa."

Blanco froze for a moment as if it took him a few seconds to register the name. His face fell and he quickly glanced in back of Mas.

"Sheezu down there." Mas gestured to the window.

Blanco rose, pulled aside his venetian blinds, and looked out into the street. The Buckwheat Beauty must have been in plain view because the former detective sank back into his swivel chair and practically snarled. "How are you connected with her?"

It was hard to explain their relationship, especially in light of Haruo and Spoon's broken engagement. "Family friend," Mas finally said. "Friend of an actual friend."

"How well do you know your friend of an actual friend?" The chair's single giant spring squeaked from below.

191

Māmā. So-so, Mas thought. But he knew that he had to imply a closer relationship or Blanco might lose interest. "Izu lookin' for dat actual friend."

"Well, your friend may be in a better place without the likes of her. She's all trouble."

Mas had expected Blanco to rant and rave a little, but nothing like this.

"Let me tell you a little something about that girl. She didn't tell you anything about her boyfriend, Estacio, did she? The local boy returns to Hanley to deal drugs?"

Mas shoved his hands in his jeans pockets.

"I didn't think so. He and Dee lived together in L.A. She got busted on drug charges, but for some reason, he went scot-free. By the mid-eighties Estacio was working solo in the valley. He was ruining the streets here. He got teenagers to make drug runs for him. Families were destroyed.

"Then Dee's father comes to Hanley to make flower deliveries. In the same town where his daughter's ex-boyfriend is running a drug empire. Is this a coincidence? Give me a break. I don't know if Estacio was threatening Dee's father or if the father wanted part of the action. But both Ike and Jorg were making cocaine runs, no doubt about it."

Blanco swallowed and brushed down one

of his sideburns. "I know you don't believe me. I barely believed it myself. But these past twenty years, I've been piecing it all together." He rose to a tall gray filing cabinet in the corner and opened the second of five drawers. "Look at all of this." The drawer sagged from the weight of manila folders and white paper. "This is all about Estacio. All the interviews I've been doing since the accident in 1986. Photographs of the crime scene. Court documents. Police reports. You know that his biological father is a well-respected politician back in Nicaragua?" He pulled out a couple of black-and-white head shots, the kind movie and sports stars have taken to autograph for their fans. One was of an older man with wavy gray hair in a three-piece suit, the other was a younger version of the former, same thin face and piercing eyes. Estacio's hair was cropped short, and instead of suit and tie, he was wearing a black shirt and jacket.

"Promo shot for a new casino in Las Vegas. Estacio was one of the VPs — that is, until he got into some trouble."

Mas was surprised that neither the Buckwheat Beauty nor Spoon had made any mention of this man. "You been talkin' to Spoon?"

"Dee's mother? She won't take my calls.

193

You know that her lawyers filed a harassment suit against me? I'm supposed to stay at least a hundred yards away from her and her daughter. I doubt the daughter even knows what's going on. She's had more relapses than Whitney Houston."

Mas didn't know who this Whitney was but gathered that the Buckwheat Beauty had been going through drug rehab like a revolving door.

"Estacio was my main target, anyway. The whole police department stayed away from him — no doubt they all were on the take. And then someone plants cocaine in my car. The DA can't prove that it's mine but the damage is done. My career's over. My marriage's over. My life's over. They think that I'm going to quit? That's not what Chuck Blanco is made of."

"Wheresu dis Estacio now?"

"Interestingly enough, he wasn't charged with a thing here in Hanley. The police just couldn't pin anything on him. Nobody would talk. Spent some time with his father in Nicaragua. But came back to Las Vegas and invested in some casinos. He was finally picked up in Arizona. It wasn't a drug violation — assault in a nightclub. Sentenced to a couple of years. He just got out a couple of weeks ago on good behavior."

Mas's ears perked up.

"Yeah, it wouldn't surprise me if Estacio had contacted Dee. Maybe he's the one who's been after those dolls."

Again, the dolls. Blanco seemed to easily read Mas's face, because he commented, "Yeah, Mrs. de Groot had called me about the dolls. I told her that I'd get them, but it was too late. That outfit in San Diego had already sold them."

"So youzu the guy makin' bids on the doll."

Blanco frowned. "Didn't get a chance to bid. They were already sold to Spoon Hayakawa."

Then who had been the competing bidder? Maybe this Estacio fellow? As Mas pulled at his shirt collar, the walls of the small wood-paneled room seemed to inch closer and closer. A bead of sweat dripped from Mas's forehead to his short-sleeved shirt.

"I've come to the conclusion that those dolls in themselves are barely worth anything. It's not what is on the outside, but the inside."

Another drop of sweat stained Mas's shirt.

"There's something in those dolls — either money or drugs. Or maybe something that connects what happened to those two men in 1986 with Estacio Pena."

Pushing a pair of reading glasses down on his nose, the former detective returned to his open filing cabinet and rifled through the manila folders. Finding what he was looking for, he tossed a couple of eight-and-a-half-by-eleven black-and-white photos on his desk.

Out of curiosity, Mas leaned forward toward the images, only to immediately regret it. One was of a burned skeleton pinned against what looked like a melted steering wheel. The other was also a charred body, this one on the side of the road. Both photos were apparently taken at night because an intense spotlight aimed at the once human subjects cast menacing, ghostly shadows.

"The death of Ike Hayakawa and Jorg de Groot was no accident," said Blanco. "At least that's what I believe. I wanted to send for a specialist to come out from Brawley. I didn't think that the fire started from the engine. I smelled gasoline all around the bodies. But my superiors and my partner at the time shot my request down.

"I really felt that this was either a warning or retribution, most likely from a gang. I'm not sure which it was. I went to Jorg's son with my theory — thought that he might be able to insist that it be investigated. He went ballistic on me! Said that it was an accident and I needed to leave it at that. Soon afterward I had to leave the force."

The weight of Blanco's pronouncements overwhelmed Mas. Was Haruo's disappearance somehow mixed up with drug gangsters? Mas felt his knees shake and then start to buckle underneath him. He reached out to the edge of the desk to steady himself.

"You can sit down," Blanco said, referring to a folding chair on the side. His voice had lost its initial edge and he sounded genuinely concerned.

"Izu go," Mas said, tentatively loosening his grip on the desk.

"No, you wait." Blanco sighed and returned to the window, which he hoisted open with the tips of his fingers. "Hey you, Hayakawa," he shouted down to the street. "Get up here and get your friend."

At that point, Mas sank into the folding chair, feeling immediate relief in his knees and legs.

Within minutes they heard the *bang-bang* of footsteps ascending the stairs. "What did you do to him?" The Buckwheat Beauty was so mad that Mas was almost flattered.

"Izu *orai*," said Mas.

Dee didn't even acknowledge Mas, now

making him question her initial reaction.

"I was telling your friend all about you and your boyfriend."

"I haven't seen him for close to twenty years."

"But you've spoken to him, haven't you? Pretty recently, I bet."

"I don't know what you're talking about." Dee attempted to keep her voice steely and strong, but both Mas and the former detective picked up on a slight faltering in her words.

"Estacio's back in Southern California."

CHAPTER TEN

There was no expression on Dee's face, aside from a rosy flush on her freckled cheeks. It was as if she had not fully absorbed Chuck Blanco's announcement that her former lover had returned to Southern California.

"You don't seem surprised." Blanco articulated Mas's thoughts.

"I'm not Estacio's keeper. I don't keep tabs on him."

"But I bet he's keeping tabs on you to get hold of those drugs dolls."

"I don't know what you're talking about." Dee lowered her gaze and her eyes fixed upon Blanco's desk: the two black-and-white photos, the ghost skeletons.

The Buckwheat Beauty dropped her mother's car keys on the floor and covered her mouth with her hands. The room became dead quiet. Mas thought that he heard a scratching through the flimsy walls. A rogue rat? Giant cockroach?

Blanco slowly removed the photos and returned them to their home in the filing cabinet. As he pushed the drawer closed, the cabinet let out a high-pitched screech during which the Buckwheat Beauty slipped out of the room.

His legs feeling much more stable, Mas rose to make his exit as well.

"I didn't mean for her to see those photos," said Blanco. "I don't trust Dee Hayakawa but I also don't think that she set her father on fire."

That seemed like the most complimentary statement the former detective could say about the Buckwheat Beauty. Mas bent down and retrieved the keys. As the attached wallet flipped open, Mas remembered the group photo with Haruo. "Dis Haruo Mukai. My friend," he said to Blanco, placing a dirty fingernail right below Haruo's face. "Heezu missin' two nights."

Blanco examined the photo for a long minute. "He actually could be any of these old-time farmers around here, except for the scar, of course. We pretty much know all of the Asians in the area, or at least we used to. There's been talk of an old Asian man who's recently been involved in the drug scene here in Imperial Valley. They call him the Chinito. Other than him, same old, same old. So this friend of yours knows Dee?"

"Suppose to marry her motha."

Blanco blinked. "Oh, I see," he said.

"First those dolls gone, then my friend."

"He didn't take them, did he? I mean, maybe that would explain his disappearance."

Why did everyone suspect Haruo of wrongdoing? Mas was actually starting to wonder about his friend as well. He tugged down on the bill of his cap before he went out the door.

"I'd take care, Mr. Arai. And if you find your friend around here, he should take care too. Strangers don't do well in Hanley, as Mr. Hayakawa and Mr. de Groot found out."

When Mas returned to the truck, the Buckwheat Beauty was in the passenger seat. Her eyes were red and swollen and Mas knew that she had been crying.

"I had to come down here with Mom to identify the body," she said after Mas climbed behind the steering wheel. "Or rather his personal belongings. His melted belt buckle. His wedding ring. They looked like they had gone through a nuclear bomb blast."

Mas stuck his key in the ignition and turned the steering wheel. He drove down the street, passing a taqueria and a donut shop. Men and women sauntered down the sidewalks, as if they were ruled by a different clock than the rest of the world.

"The police said that we didn't have to see the actual body — unrecognizable. This was the first time I've seen those photos."

Mas didn't know what to think. He had come to Imperial Valley for answers, but he was only more confused. Did the daughter have some kind of angle? It was obvious that this Chuck Blanco suspected the daughter of some kind of complicity, wrongdoing. Why hadn't she spoken of this Estacio Pena before? Mas didn't understand their relationship — she certainly didn't refute knowing him in some capacity. Maybe that's why she was sticking so close to Mas, to ensure that he wouldn't be straying too close to the truth.

"Your Mexican friend callsu you," Mas finally said rather than asked.

The Buckwheat Beauty bit down on the insides of her cheeks. "Okay," she finally said, "Estacio did get in touch with me after getting released. But I told him that I never wanted to hear from him again. I swear. I didn't say anything to you because I didn't want my mother to know. She would have been devastated. I've never spoken Estacio's name to her since Daddy's death."

"Blanco saysu your daddy may have been killed."

Dee's face darkened. "He claims that some drug dealers were trying to scare me off from testifying against Estacio. Only problem is, no one was threatening. I didn't know anything, so there was nothing to tell. And by the way, Estacio is not Mexican, okay? He was born here. His father is from Nicaragua."

Mas didn't care about Estacio's personal history or citizenship, just if he was involved in Haruo's disappearance in some way.

Mas got back on the highway. The sun was now ablaze, and the inside of the Ford sweltered like a tin oven. Sweat dripped from the heads of the truck's two passengers. Mas finally placed his soaked cap on the seat as hot air from the open window blew on his earlobes and through his thinning hair.

The emotion of the day must have weighed heavily on Dee, because she was already nodding off. It was just as well because Mas needed to take a detour through Niland without dealing with any prying questions.

As the Ford shook from the bumps in the highway, Mas couldn't help but be mad at Haruo for falling for this mother-and-daughter charade. There was Spoon, locking up her secrets, and then here was Dee, holding back the truth. Even more than ever, Mas had to find his friend to tell him what a *bakatare,* a stupid fool, he had been.

But what if Haruo could not be found? Mas desperately searched the landscape as if the earth could talk to him. Bunches of clouds gathered above like stuffing torn out of a pillow. The skyline made Mas's gut shrivel into loneliness. All he heard was that nature, like man, could be both beautiful and brutal.

He drove past an irrigation ditch half full of water and then furrows of dirt being prepared for spring planting. He wasn't on the lookout for fresh produce, but rocks. Rocks didn't come easy in L.A. — not unless you were willing to shell out some serious dough. And while Mas was consumed with worry about Haruo, there was still one sliver of his heart that was reserved for Genessee Howard.

The land was barren and dry, no signs or demarcations of the farm where Mas used to work. Mas had gone there with a gang of other Kibei men, those virtually without a country. They slept together in chicken-coop shacks and worked alongside Filipino men — some younger and others older bachelors. A couple of the Filipinos had even fought for America during World War Two and were citing promises from the U.S. government, "We can become citizens now," only to later discover that those promises were easily broken. All of them worked from sunrise to sunset, six days a week, but it had not been a chore for the teenaged Mas. He didn't mind hard work; he actually craved it. And there was always time in between to learn to throw a football and watch the Filipino men dig underground pits for the most delicious pork barbecue.

Spying a small pile of rocks, Mas pulled over to the side of the road. There were some pieces of sandstone, jagged and broken like decaying teeth. These shards had no sense of peace or wholeness, their place was here in a desolate and abandoned land, not in the backyard of a retired music professor seeking rest. After studying the empty horizon, Mas got back into the truck and drove home, the sleeping Buckwheat Beauty in the passenger seat occasionally crying out unintelligibly with each unexpected pothole and turn in the road.

■ ■ ■ ■

As soon as Mas had returned home from dropping Dee off at her sister's house, the phone rang. Apparently one or even two days of a missing Haruo didn't command his children's attention, but seventy-two hours set off a red flag. Funny thing was Mas thought the daughter, Kimiyi, would be the one to come around first, but it turned out that it was the *botchan,* the mama's boy.

"Did he show up at your house?" Clement asked.

Mas told him no.

"It was a pupil-free day at my school," Clement explained, "so I went to the racetrack to talk to his old cronies. They told me that they had seen him wandering around the track last week, but he didn't seem to be placing any bets."

The son had covered the same ground as Mas had two days ago, but with a much bigger payoff. Clement was a PE teacher and basketball coach at a local high school and was apparently quite adept at moving around. He also, unfortunately, had more practice chasing down his father during his more desperate days. And the search this time hadn't ended with the track.

"Also spoke to Taxie this morning. I heard about that retired guy who was found dead at the market," said Clement. "You don't think that incident has anything to do with my father, do you?"

Mas didn't answer because there was no definitive answer to give.

"He wasn't at work again. My father's a lot of things, but he always shows up for work. Even when he disappeared from the house for weeks, he always made sure his customers were taken care of." Mas heard a slight tenor of desperation in the son's voice. Normally it would have annoyed Mas, but today it came as a relief. Someone else was worried about Haruo. So when Clement asked to meet Mas at the flower market the next morning for a late breakfast, Mas didn't hesitate to say yes.

Chizuko had been a *kyōiku-mama,* an education mom who stayed up with Mari as she labored on her homework. Mas himself had never been much of a student. But some of Chizuko's passion must have rubbed off on him over the years, because he knew that he had to do some of his own homework before meeting Clement the next day.

For instance, had Haruo possibly stolen

the dolls? If he had, where would he have sold them? He figured a downtown pawn-shop would have no idea what to do with Japanese dolls.

As he was mulling this possibility over a bowl of boiled instant ramen, he read the latest issue of the *Rafu Shimpo* newspaper. And there, hidden underneath the column "Horse's Mouth," was an announcement that a *ningyō* exhibition was coming this weekend to Little Tokyo, compliments of the nation's only certified Japanese doll-making instructor.

Any sensei worth her salt would be at the community center gallery all day and night to make sure that every detail was attended to. It was not *guzen,* a simple accident, that he'd come across the article. To have that plus Clement's involvement was a trace of good news in days of bad.

Mas's hunch about the sensei's work ethic was on target. When he arrived at the Little Tokyo community and cultural center, which incidentally housed the Japanese garden where Spoon and Haruo were sup-posed to have had their nuptials, a roly-poly Japanese woman shaped like a Russian nest-ing doll was already there in the gallery. Her dolls were on display, but the glass doors

208

were locked, so when Mas rapped on the surface, the sensei almost swirled around in a full circle in surprise.

Los Angeles's Little Tokyo had indeed recently experienced a face-lift, with new businesses catering to a young, hip, tattooed crowd, but there was still a less-moneyed edginess to the area that, like fog, was most apparent at night and early morning.

The sensei furrowed her brow as if to discern whether Mas might be friend or foe. Mas was glad that he had showered before coming and that Three Flowers oil had been applied to the furrows of graying hair on his head.

"Nandesuka?" the woman asked in Japanese through the locked glass door.

"Chotto," just a little thing Mas needed to say. Mas knew that this was woman's talk, but here in the United States, men often mixed male with female expressions. Made sense as the mamas were often the ones controlling all the talk in the American household.

Somehow the mention of *chotto* did its magic. The sensei unlocked the upper dead bolt, but her face was still guarded.

"You numba one sensei in *ningyō,* I hear."

Hearing number one, *ichiban,* was a salve to the woman's ego. She bowed to receive

209

the compliment and stepped back to allow Mas inside the gallery.

"*Sugoi,*" Mas said, gazing at the assortment of dolls. He was not exaggerating. He was truly impressed with the riches on display. The realistic faces on a young kimono-clad ingenue, the young daimyo during the samurai times, the long-haired Ainu girls in simple embroidered costumes.

"I make them all by hand," she said proudly. "Six thousand strands of silk thread applied with a needle." She pointed to the Ainu dancers.

Mas had thought his work as a gardener was tedious at times. But doll making put his efforts of detail to shame.

The sensei explained how she mixed a pulverized oyster shell powder from Japan with fine rice gruel to make her clay. With this lightweight clay, she formed the face with her fingers, and when it hardened, she chiseled the surface with delicate knives and tools.

What if she made a mistake and created a face that she didn't quite like? Would she abandon the project or start all over?

The sensei puckered her ample lips. "Oh, no, *kawaiiso.*"

She would feel too sad to destroy the misshapen face. This sensei was cut from the same cloth as the strange proprietor of Hina House. Not only had the dolls taken on human form, they also had full emotions and personalities.

Mas approached one of the dolls, which sported fringes of eyelashes that no doubt the sensei had fastened one lash at a time. "How much?" he asked in Japanese.

"Sell? Oh, no. I cannot sell."

"You neva sell?"

"Well, one time, *ne.* This Beverly Hills woman came to one of my doll shows. Offered eight thousand dollars."

Mas straightened his back. Sonafugun. He thought Spoon's three thousand was exorbitant, but eight thousand? The sensei explained that the doll had been large — the *hakujin* seemed to think the bigger, the better. But that one sale had been an anomaly.

You see, she said, rather than being *tanoshimi,* an enjoyment, doll making for her was racked with *kurushimi.*

Suffering? Mas widened his eyes. In all his seventy-odd years, he never thought a hobby would engender such pain. He himself was drawn to gambling because he loved that soaring shot of excitement, the blinding bolt that hit the bottom of your spine and spread up to your skull. Yes, when you drew bad cards or made a bad bet, your emotions went downhill, but you always believed that your luck would change. In fact, chronic gamblers quickly forgot their losses, because if you didn't, you wouldn't bother to return to the tables.

"Kurushii," the sensei repeated. The birth of the dolls, like children, was marked by suffering. But it was precisely that suffering that made dolls so precious.

Mas asked about *hina* dolls, which apparently fell in a different category from the dolls she made.

"If you want to know about *hina ningyō,* go to San Diego."

"Hina House," Mas said.

"Hai, hai." The roly-poly woman rocked her head. If anyone wanted information about a *hina* doll in the mainland United States, the first place anyone would go would be there.

Mas kept that in the back of his mind as he drove a few blocks south to the flower market. He wasn't quite sure what he could say to Clement. In fact, he hadn't seen the son since perhaps Haruo's divorce a couple of decades ago.

Even back then, Clement wasn't one to mince words, and that hadn't changed. "I don't hate my dad," he said. "I just blame him for breaking up my family." He took some vigorous bites of his pancakes and swallowed. "I was still in high school, you know. I saw what the gambling did to my mother. My sister was shielded to some respect. I'm the one who had to pick up the pieces. That's why I had to go to community college first for a couple of years and went into education instead of getting into something more moneymaking."

So was the son saying teaching PE and coaching wasn't his first choice of a profession? With his boxy shoulders and strong arms (inherited from the mother and not the father, for sure), Clement was built to use his body, not his head. Mas couldn't imagine what other line of work he could have pursued.

"But I'm still not saying that I hate him," Clement repeated while Mas added more ketchup to his scrambled eggs.

Since it was Saturday, the small coffeehouse attached to the market was not crowded. It only seemed that way, compliments of mirrored panels installed along the south wall. So the men in the two booths in the back magically doubled without two times the noise. Fine with Mas, who was starting to have some problems with his hearing of late.

The west side of the restaurant, in contrast to the main dining floor, was full of windows, making Mas feel a little more human. With the one exception of sitting inside a Las Vegas casino for hours on end, Mas would usually wilt without having the sun on his back for at least a good portion of the day.

Clement continued his list of things his father failed to do. Mas didn't know how this was going to help them find Haruo, but if he had to swallow this bitter pill, he would. Eventually sensing the presence of someone standing beside them, he welcomed any kind of interruption from listening to the litany of Haruo's sins.

"Hey, Mas." The Buckwheat Beauty, looking much more rested (probably from all that napping in the car). Her hair was tied up in a ponytail and she was wearing a T-shirt much too big for her body, most likely her sister's.

"Hallo," Mas greeted back. Even though they had spent the whole day Friday together, he still didn't expect Dee to be so friendly. He then remembered Clement and offered nameless introductions: "Dis Haruo's son. Dis Spoon's daughter."

"Oh," they both said and averted their eyes.

What had contributed to their mutual shyness — that they came that close to becoming stepsister and stepbrother?

"Well, anyway, I saw you when I was getting some coffee, so I thought I'd say hi —"

Before Dee could leave with her take-out coffee, she was approached by a man from one of the back booths. His thinning blond hair was so light that it was almost invisible. Standing at least six feet tall, he had a thick neck and chest, accentuated by his undersized green polo shirt that read DE GROOT'S BIRDS-OF-PARADISE. It might as well have read JORG DE GROOT'S SON, because it was clear who he was.

"What the hell were you doing in Hanley yesterday?" he asked.

Dee frowned, squeezing her paper cup of coffee. "And good morning to you too, Geoff."

How did Jorg's boy know about their investigative trip? Dee must have spilled the beans to one of her coworkers, Mas figured.

"My mother's scared shitless because of you."

"Well, sorry to hear that, but I don't know what you're talking about."

"Chuck Blanco was killed last night. Not sure exactly how — the police aren't saying — but it happened right inside his house."

CHAPTER ELEVEN

"What?" Dee placed her coffee cup on the edge of the table at the flower market café. "I don't believe it."

Mas's heart pounded fast and furious. How did Geoff de Groot even know about Chuck Blanco's demise? Once Dee composed herself, that was her question as well. "How did you hear this?"

"The Hanley cops called us. Apparently my mother was the last person Blanco talked to on the phone. He wanted to know why you were in Hanley with some old Japanese guy."

Mas's stomach turned, once, twice, and then three times over. He hoped that Geoff wasn't looking at him now.

"We were looking for my mom's ex-fiancé. He's missing."

"And you think he's over in Hanley? Why?"

"It was just a lead, okay? I was just trying

to find out the truth. And trying to find those dolls."

"And so where are those dolls, Dee?"

"What are you trying to say?"

"You know what I'm saying. What pawn-shop are they in now?"

"I didn't take them. I'm trying to find them, dammit." Dee balled her fists, and Mas winced at the faint yet distinct scars on her lower arms.

"Nice cover, Dee, really nice. I like your new superhero identity. Even my mother halfway believes you've gone straight. But not me. I know better."

"You know nothing about me. You haven't said two words to me since I've come back."

"What's there to say? How long is it going to be until you're back on Skid Row, begging for dime bags? How long will it be before you break your mother's heart again?"

The men in the back booths had now turned completely around to witness de Groot's drubbing of Dee. Pico's face — still no Roberto — was rapt, as if viewing a prize boxing match. Even the Asian waitresses peered out worriedly from behind the pastry display, perhaps imagining dishes flying at any moment.

It was no surprise when their harsh exchange escalated into an obscenity-laden shouting match. Mas thought that he should do something, but luckily Clement stepped in.

"Okay, okay." He stood up and spread out his thick arms as if he were a referee. His intervention silenced Dee for a moment but seemed to further aggravate de Groot's son.

"You know this woman? My father died because of her. That was twenty years ago. And my mother still has to suffer because of her gangster friends."

Dee pulled de Groot's son away from their audience. She lowered her voice, but Mas and Clement could still hear their conversation. "I had nothing to do with that crash. My father died too, you know."

"But why were they down there in the first place, Dee? Your empty head has never put that together. There was no need for them to be in Imperial Valley. They were on a drug run — to protect you, get that ex-boyfriend off your back. Your dad, always the John Wayne, the man wearing the white hat. And my dad right beside him because he didn't know any better."

"You have no proof."

"I saw the money with my own eyes. Stacks of bills, must have been hundreds of thousands of dollars. My dad didn't mean for me to see, to know. But I did. And you know my dad, he wasn't one to say two words to anyone, including me, but he told me that he and Uncle Ike had a job to do. That I needed to trust him and not say anything to anybody. And that I was in my twenties, a man now." The large man's voice cracked, causing Mas to look up in surprise. "It was almost as if he knew that he was going to die soon.

"So even after they were killed, I didn't say anything about the money. I wasn't going to let anyone think my dad was some sort of criminal. I knew that he had his reasons. But now when my mother comes to me all upset because some lowlifes are harassing her, I can't keep quiet. This has to stop. You tell your boyfriend and his homies or whatever you call them to back off or I'll go after them myself."

Dee stood frozen, much like the way she responded to her confrontation with Blanco. Mas began to notice a pattern. The Buckwheat Beauty was hot and fiery as a coal-burning train engine in the beginning of a fight, but she inevitably lost fuel, stopped in her tracks, and then finally hightailed it in the opposite direction. And here she did it again, as she escaped through the street entrance of the coffeehouse.

Just able to see the top of her head through the windows as she ran north, Mas wanted to go after the Buckwheat Beauty. But his more Japanese male side kept him tethered to his chair. After all, what did he know of Dee Hayakawa? Yes, they had spent a good amount of time together yesterday, when he had experienced her softness and vulnerability. But he didn't surrender all the reservations he had about the girl. Haruo, after all, had been the main purpose for their long drive to Hanley, and they returned empty-handed. Until Mas dug out the truth of Dee's connection with this Estacio Pena, her actions still remained suspect.

De Groot's son, whose knotted hands had been on his belt the whole time, lowered his arms, as if his gunfight had ended. He then shook his head and rejoined his breakfast mates.

Clement, meanwhile, had pushed away his plate, and Mas felt like doing the same. The conflict had robbed them of their appetite. "Do you think that my father's caught in the crosshairs of this?" Clement murmured. "I mean, what kind of family was he marrying into?"

"Sheezu *orai*. Just sick in a way." *A little like your father Haruo and his gambling* byoki, Mas thought to himself.

"I've spoken to the police about my dad's disappearance, and some officers may be coming to the market to do interviews. They want to talk to you again to go over some facts."

Mas readily agreed.

"Kiyomi and I plan to offer a reward. I'm prepared to do anything, even hire a private investigator."

"You gotta do whatsu you gotta do," said Mas, both relieved and a little hurt that his own detecting efforts had not been acknowledged. But Haruo was more than three days missing, and now hearing about Chuck Blanco's death had certainly shaken Mas. This was no time for *shirōto,* amateurs. It was time to bring in the professionals.

Mas sat by himself at the table for another half an hour, picking at his cold ketchup-smeared scrambled eggs and rubbery sausage. He thought maybe if he waited long enough, the Buckwheat Beauty would reappear. She hadn't done anything drastic, had she?

Mas couldn't believe that Chuck Blanco had been killed apparently only a few hours after they had seen him face-to-face. Mas couldn't help feeling somewhat responsible. After all, it had been his idea to go to Hanley. But the town did have a few remnants of the Wild West. Couldn't it be that the attack on Blanco had nothing to do with their visit?

Haruo's son was gone, leaving a crisp twenty-dollar bill to cover both his and Mas's breakfasts. Normally Mas would have objected and insisted on paying the entire bill instead. But that morning's excitement had distracted him from his sense of propriety.

Soon after Clement left, so did de Groot's son. Geoff de Groot had been rough, too rough, thought Mas. Sure, Dee's former connections had been *kitanai,* downright dirty, but she was making herself over. At what point could a person finally let go of how she used to be? And when would people allow her to do so? De Groot's and Dee's absence now cleared the way for gossip of the most vicious kind — tall tales that took place in lawn mower shops, nurseries, and backroom poker games.

"Man, Geoff really went off on her. I've never seen him that mad," Mas heard one of the men in the back of the restaurant say.

"He's been on edge a lot. It got even worse when they found Casey's body."

"Geoff never got along with Casey, huh?"

"Yeah, it goes way, way back. I think after

Geoff's dad died."

"Casey must have done something stupid."

"Wasn't he trying to horn in on the deal in Imperial Valley? You were around at that time, Pico. What do you remember?"

"Nothing. I see nothing, hear nothing, speak nothing." The familiar voice.

"That's a new one." The whole table erupted in laughter.

"All I know is Geoff won't give a damn cent toward the funeral moneys we're collecting for Casey."

"That's messed up."

"Hey, guys, it's a free country. At least Geoff isn't a hypocrite. He didn't like Casey and ain't going to pretend that he did now."

A couple of the men, including Pico, left the table, leaving a still healthy share of gossipmongers.

"Hard to believe that they once were together."

"What?"

"Dee and Geoff."

"You've got to be kiddin' me."

"It was a long time ago, when they were in junior high school."

"The last time she was clean, I bet."

A few of the men laughed.

A new voice thankfully spoke out: "I think she's a lot better now."

"Maybe, maybe not."

Mas loudly cleared his throat and spat on his cold eggs. He covered the remains of his breakfast with a wadded-up napkin. The men in the back grew suspiciously quiet as Mas left a few extra dollars on the table for a tip and went out the door to the street.

Going north meant a few steps closer to Skid Row, and that was the direction the Buckwheat Beauty seemed to have gone. Following the trail of empty syringes and the stink of urine, he wondered if she had entered a den of temptation. Mas himself had been an addict of tobacco for more than fifty years before he quit cold turkey upon spending time with his grandson in New York. It was precisely these times of stress when an addict craved his or her poison. That's why his fingers imagined bringing a cigarette to his lips. And most likely, that's what the Buckwheat Beauty was feeling right now about her drug of choice.

Mas stood on a corner, searching for Dee's thin frame in her oversized T-shirt. A huge black man in a wig and shiny green dress mumbled some words his way, and Mas put on a *shirankao,* a blank face that pretended to be completely unaware.

Mas limited his contact with Skid Row residents as much as he could. He definitely did not look any of them in the eye. But there were times when he had to drive into the Gardeners' Federation in Toytown to buy some fertilizer or a twenty-pound bag of rice harvested fresh from the San Joaquin Valley, or maybe reconcile his bill for his federation-sponsored medical insurance. That's when he ran into some homeless men who expertly guided him through the maze of delivery trucks, boxes from China being carted on dollies, and sedans driven by discount seekers. This was the only time he would poke his hand in his pocket for any loose change to give to his homeless guide. They were regulars, after all, offering a service. Mas admired any fellows seeking to be entrepreneurial, as long as they didn't touch the Ford.

Through the crowd of the walking dead, Mas spied a familiar figure. The man was short, maybe only a few inches taller than Mas. Roberto of El Salvador, the man who was supposed to be wiping the brow of his sick mother. What was he doing here in Los Angeles, and Skid Row in particular?

Mas began to follow Roberto, curious what the flower market worker would find of interest in Skid Row. With the gentrification of industrial buildings, the homeless quadrant had certainly shrunk into a tight ball that was threatening to unravel and implode at any time. And Roberto, his new tour guide, was leading Mas right into the thick of it.

Roberto entered a park through a tall green iron fence. Outside the fence was a full-scale one-person toilet, operational only with the insertion of a quarter. Looked and smelled like most people opted to forgo the fancy toilet and save their quarters for more nefarious purposes.

Every inch of the park seemed to be taken up by people — no blade of green grass in sight. To have wall-to-wall people in this tiny space, a human zoo, or perhaps even worse, a detention camp, made Mas feel woozy and sick. The smell was full of humanity — layers of *shikko* and *unko* and sweat and vomit and body odor. It seemed to have soaked through the concrete and maybe even the air.

No one seemed to leer at or pay attention to Mas, as if he looked like he belonged. In his search for Roberto, Mas, for the first time, had to look into the faces of the homeless. Among the predominantly black and brown population were women with children, sometimes more than one or even two in tow. A few Asian and *hakujin* men who looked in their thirties or forties, their bodies beaten down by drugs.

And then the slim triangle of an elbow — was that the Buckwheat Beauty? Mas squeezed through the crowd, feeling damp, dirt-caked jackets brush against his face.

By the jungle gym, underneath the swing set, he spied Dee and a man who stood only a few inches taller than her. He had a slight build that complemented his fancy black leather jacket and high-tone slacks. His curly dark hair was cropped short, and in the spring sun, something bright glinted off of his earlobe. It was from a distance, but Mas still felt that he had made a match. The man talking to Dee owned the face that was featured in one of the late Chuck Blanco's black-and-white glossy photos.

"You interested in girls?" A black man who looked to be in his fifties sat on a red plastic vegetable crate at the side of the entrance. He wore a fishing cap and his hair was twisted in long dreadlocks.

Mas shook his head.

The man tilted his head back against the iron gate. "That one's not hookin'."

Mas frowned.

"I know her. I've seen her before. She's not hookin', I tell you."

"You know dat man she talkin' to?"

"What, you some kind of cop?" The man weighed what stood in front of him and then grinned. "You must be her old man."

"They buddy-buddy?" Mas asked more emphatically.

"Hold on. Hold on." The man narrowed his eyes. He leaned forward on his crate, almost tipping it over. "All questions will be answered with a little green."

Mas inflated his cheeks with air. Luckily he had a ten and a five smashed in his pocket (no opening of his wallet in this place), which he scooped out in one handful.

The man took the money and gave him something in return — an empty, dirty plastic bag.

The man winked. "Don't want anyone thinking I'm sellin' information," he whispered. His breath was harsh, not necessarily bad but laced with the scent of something salty and oily like olives.

"Anyway, I first sees the girl about a couple of days ago. I mean around here she kind of stands out, you know what I'm sayin'? She's no Miss America on the outside, but she can be one in here. I was thinkin' that maybe she was new and drummin' up some new customers, you know

228

what I'm sayin'? But then I see who she's after. The Prince, that's what we've been calling him. Turns out he was known here about twenty years ago, made his fortune, and ran away to Las Vegas."

The same snippets that Chuck Blanco had reported.

"He's a poser, if you ask me. I guess his father back in Mexico or wherever he's from was a big deal. Prince said that he had the U.S. government down on its knees. But why's he back here now, that's what I want to know. Seems a little soft."

The two didn't seem to be too cozy. Dee was in fact hugging her chest with her arms, creating a barrier from Estacio. He grasped her hand and squeezed something into her palm. She tried to return it, but he merely shook his head and laughed.

A black limousine pulled up to the side of the gate and honked its horn. The extravagant ride was apparently for Estacio because he tipped his hand toward Dee before sauntering toward the car.

In the meantime, the gatekeeper had shuffled away with his red crate, and in fact, other homeless men and women cleared away from Mas so that he was surrounded by a moat of empty space — enough to attract the Buckwheat Beauty's attention. Her eyes, focused on Mas, grew big. He knew what she was thinking: What the hell are you doing here? She took off like a rocket and Mas got firsthand experience of how fast that skinny body could move.

The ground near the gate was littered with syringes and flattened fast-food cups. Farther down by a wall sat a line of people who had set up their temporary homes. Refrigerator boxes, grocery carts filled with tied plastic bags, patched tents, and even suitcases on wheels.

On the opposite corner Mas recognized Roberto again. He was talking to a gigantic black man, the same one that seemed to be mourning Casey's demise a day after his body had been found in the alley behind the market. The man kept shaking his enormous head back and forth. He didn't seem angry, just annoyed.

Mas would have crossed over to confront Roberto, but that would deter him from his hunt for the Buckwheat Beauty. He jogged until he felt sharp pain in his joints. Placing his hands on his thighs, he sucked in deep breaths of polluted air. It took him a good half hour to finally reach the second-floor flower market parking lot.

Since it was way past the market's closing time, the lot was virtually empty aside from his Ford on one side and the Hayakawa family delivery truck on the other. He saw no human form but heard some soft meowing on the Hayakawa side. As he approached the delivery truck, the cries got louder and louder, but still no sign of anything living. He finally bent down, releasing popping sounds from his knees, and looked underneath the truck only to spot familiar Converse high-tops.

Walking around the truck helped to solve the mystery. The two alley cats were sitting in the Buckwheat Beauty's lap, licking tears off of her chin. Seated on the floor, she leaned against the tire well, getting the right side of her sister's shirt soiled with grime from the street.

Mas had been all set to shout at her — What were you doing with Estacio Pena? — but it wasn't the right time. Instead of speaking, he placed his hand on her head. Slowly, slowly, her chin came up, revealing swollen eyes filled with tears, the freckles even more noticeable when wet. "Poor cats," she said. "They're starving without Haruo."

Her right hand was tightened into a fist and Mas gently tugged at her fingers until she finally opened her hand. Some white powder in the tip of a plastic bag, still secured by a twist tie.

"Cocaine," Mas murmured, taking the bag from her palm.

"It's not cocaine. Heroin."

Heroin. Haruo had said that *hiropon* had been the drug of the past, but in fact, it seemed to be making its way back in popularity.

Seven months of being straight, isn't that what the girl said? At the time Mas belittled her achievements in his mind but now seeing what went on in the hell park, he had to admire anyone who could scratch her way out of that lifestyle.

"I was this close, Mas, this close." Her empty palm was trembling. "But I started thinking about my dad. About how he may have died trying to protect me. I couldn't dishonor his memory again."

CHAPTER TWELVE

Kin no byobu ni utsuruhi o
Kasukani yusuru haru no kaze
Sukoshi shirozake mesaretaka
Akai okao no udaijin

Light reflecting on the gold screen
Faintly flickers from the spring breeze
Did you have some rice wine?
Red-faced dignitary
— "Hina Matsuri Song," third stanza

As Mas drove the Buckwheat Beauty to her group meeting at the rehab facility, she and the Ford took turns sighing. First was the truck at a stoplight on Wilshire near Mac-Arthur Park — a faint squeal emanating from under the hood — and then came Dee, a deep, wheezy breath as they passed the homeless men and women seated at the edge of the urban lake.

Mas was happy that he found the girl

before she had a chance to relapse, but it was obvious that her mind, if not her body, had gone underground to her drug-abusing days. "I need to be in group," she said to Mas, and he, not even fully understanding, agreed to drive her wherever help could be found.

Group turned out to be in a residential drug treatment facility in South Los Angeles, apparently started by low-level ex-gangsters and Yellow Power activists of the 1970s. Mas drove through the parking lot and braked by the door.

"You can drop me off here, Mas," she said. "I'll call my sister to pick me up later." Dee did not move from her seat, and for a minute, Mas was worried that she might make a scene. But she actually was in the mood for confessing: "I have to tell you something before you leave."

Mas turned off the engine, but his hands remained wrapped around the steering wheel, bracing himself for what surprises might come next.

"I did date Estacio once upon a time," she said. "We actually lived together." She explained that Estacio was his given name but not the one that he first went by. "When I met him, he was Steve. He was actually born and raised in Imperial Valley by his mom, who's white. While we were together, he went to Nicaragua to meet his dad — who was some kind of political leader — for the first time. He came back as Estacio with a new line of work.

"We were both in the music scene and did our share of drugs. But now Steve-Estacio had a new supply of drugs — powerful stuff, pure stuff. I didn't really know what he was doing. That's what I told the police, anyway. We were living in East Hollywood at the time, and the police burst in one morning. We were in bed and Estacio was out the window in two seconds flat. And there I was, all by myself. They found a kilo of cocaine hidden all over the house. In electrical outlets, the toilet tank, lamps. I was arrested and sent to the women's jail. I didn't know what to do, so I had to call my parents. I broke their hearts that day — I mean, really broke them. They went to my arraignment and then mortgaged the business to put up my bail."

"Dis Estacio —"

"Was suddenly nowhere. He had disappeared. I knew of a lawyer who he had used in the past and he wouldn't tell me anything. Now looking back, it was a good thing that he disappeared like that on me."

Mas tightened his grip on the steering

wheel, digging his fingernails into his palms.

"I didn't know anything about Estacio going back to Imperial Valley. But, anyway, suddenly the DA offers me this sweetheart deal. I go into treatment, I'll be on probation but no jail time. So I jump at it.

"I've fallen down a couple of times these past twenty years. I got married to a guy who used to be a lot of fun when he was high and then he was high all the time without any of the fun. I finally split up with him a year ago, and here I am now, back home with Mom but clean, barely. I've made a lot of bad decisions, but I'm really trying to change."

Mas didn't doubt the Buckwheat Beauty, although he had plenty of reasons to do so.

"Whatsu dis guy, Estacio, want dis time?"

"He came to the market a few days ago and my mom was there in our stall. I told him to meet me at San Julian Park — figured no one from the market would be there. Estacio tells me how his father is a very well-respected man in Nicaragua right now and how Estacio himself has two kids in elementary school back there. I don't give a rat's ass and I tell him as much. He tells me that his father all last year had been getting these strange anonymous postcards with this weird writing. Some

236

secret message, I guess, I don't know. Anyway, the father is all freaked out and was waiting for Estacio to get out of the slammer to do something about it. 'What does this have to do with me?' I ask him. 'Just wondering if you heard anything,' he says. Then, in passing, he starts asking me about Jorg de Groot. Mr. de Groot, he might have met him once outside my parents' house. So why is he asking me about him? He wants to know if I heard anything about Mr. de Groot lately. 'You know that he's dead,' I tell him. 'Yeah,' he says, 'but I heard that he had left something behind in some safe-deposit box.' This was a couple of days after the dolls had been stolen from our house. I tell him nothing. I figure that he's looking for money or who knows what. But the dolls? Those have nothing to do with him. So I tell him nothing about the dolls and that I don't want to ever see him again."

Dee laced her fingers together in her lap as if she were a schoolgirl back in the classroom. "So, yeah, I knew Estacio. And yeah, he was my boyfriend. But that was a lifetime ago. Has nothing to do with me now. But guys like Estacio, no matter how many times you wash your hands, their stink somehow stays with you. I mean, we're talking twenty years ago, and I'm still paying for it."

But why had she met with him today? Mas asked.

"He wanted to know about you."

"He say my name?"

"He first described you as an older Japanese man. And then he mentioned your name, Masao Arai."

"Masao?" Other than the United States government, his mother and wife were the only ones who called Mas by his full name. He had not said his full name to Blanco, so how had Estacio Pena possibly known it? The back of Mas's neck felt itchy, as if a spider were crawling down his shirt collar.

Dee turned directly to Mas. "I'm sorry I didn't tell you the whole story before, but I didn't want to bring it up again. If I thought any of this would have helped you find Haruo, I would have told you everything from the start."

Upon hearing Haruo's name, Mas felt a short pain stab his gut. It had been four full days since anyone had laid eyes on Haruo. Four days was more than enough time for someone to drive to Vegas, blow his wad, and come back to L.A. penniless. But still no sign of Haruo. Mas tried not to think about Chuck Blanco's demise, because if the missing *hina* dolls had led to one man's death, they certainly could be connected to another.

Mas had a last question for Dee before she left for group. It was a strange one, he knew, but she seemed unfazed that he was inquiring about her father's dental care.

After answering, she hopped out of the car and headed for the two-story building. Before she opened the door, she abruptly turned around, to make sure that Mas was still there, watching. In her oversized clothing but more so with her facial expression, she transformed into that young girl needing her father to prod her on, assure her that she would be okay on her own.

The Ford's motor was still running, so Mas quickly made a U-turn to head out. He was relieved that the Buckwheat Beauty was getting help, but he also realized that he was no closer to finding Haruo. Clement was now in charge of the search party, but Mas couldn't just sit back and drink Budweisers and play solitaire. Too bad he had so few customers. In the past, work had been a great diversion from pain and worry.

Mas realized that he was only about a few miles away from Genessee Howard's house in Mid-City. He was without any rocks but still had some ideas for the rock garden in his head. Suddenly he wanted nothing more than to sit in Genessee's warm kitchen with a cup of coffee in a handmade mug.

When he arrived at Genessee's street, he knew he had made a mistake. Just like the incident at Dr. Svelick's, there was a huge warning sign in front of the house — only this wasn't a white Toyota truck but a brown Chevy van. On the porch bench sat Genessee, and right next to her was the older black gardener Mas had seen the last time on the street.

Before Mas could speed away, Genessee waved to him and got to her feet.

Sonafugun, thought Mas. It was too late for him to make his getaway. Mas parked in front of the van and, straightening his Dodgers cap, got out of the Ford.

"Mas, what a wonderful surprise," she called out.

The gardener beside her also rose. He was wearing a jumpsuit that read HENRY'S GAR-DEN on his left chest. In his hands were a mug, the same handmade rustic one Mas had drunk from before. Together they looked like a perfectly matched couple. Mas wished that he could disappear.

"This is Henry, my regular gardener. Henry, this is Mas Arai, the one who suggested the rock garden."

"Pleased to meet you." Henry held out a calloused hand, and Mas gripped it with his. Normally Mas would be embarrassed at how torn up his palms and fingernails were, but today he wore his blisters as a badge of honor. Only problem was Henry's hands seemed even more calloused from work.

"Perfect timing, Mas, because Henry just delivered an unbelievable gift." She pulled at the cuff of Mas's sleeve and he resisted the impulse to clasp her free hand. She led him into the backyard, where a mound of smooth stones had been dumped into the former dirt bike course.

Anyone who didn't know about rocks wouldn't think much of a pile of them. But looking at Henry's gift, Mas saw dollar signs. Each stone must be worth a dollar, and there must have been five hundred in Genessee's backyard.

"One of my other clients was getting rid of her Japanese garden to grow vegetables," explained Henry. "She said that I could get all the rocks free as long as I took care of carting them away."

"Yah, yah, very good," Mas commented, jealousy burning his neck. He was the one who came up with the rock garden idea. He was supposed to bring Zen to Genessee Howard's life, only to find that he had been bested by a gardener named Henry.

"Well, I betta go."

"Already, Mas? No, stay for some coffee. I can make a fresh pot."

Mas, who had taken off his Dodgers cap to fully absorb the treasure of the rocks, put it back on his head.

Genessee followed Mas down her cement pathway while Henry the gardener remained on the porch. "Are you all right, Mas? You haven't told me why you stopped by."

Mas merely shook his head as if to say good-bye and jogged across the street, his elbows pointed out like chicken wings. Back in the truck and driving, he cursed himself. *Bakatare, bakatare.* At each stop, the Ford sighed, so Mas cursed it too. They were two fools on the road in L.A. How could Mas even imagine that he was more than he was — a has-been good-for-nothing gardener who was just counting days before Lopez, Sing, and Iwasaki Mortuary would be making arrangements to lower his ashes into the ground.

His thoughts returned to the Buckwheat Beauty, in her oversized T-shirt and her high-top tennis shoes. What was she doing now in her group? Sniveling and crying, no doubt, telling how she had been that close to snorting, swallowing, smoking, whatever they did with *hiropon* these days. How wonderful it would be to escape and forget with either drugs or a group. Then Mas could be freed from all worry, all *shinpai,* about Haruo.

Why was Haruo taken from Mas's house, anyway? One theory was that he could have been followed — it was common knowledge at the market that he was staying at Mas's house. Or else it could be that Haruo had not been the intended target at all. In spite of Haruo's scar, Mas could pass for Haruo at a distance. Instead of snatching Haruo, did the kidnappers hope to get Mas?

But who would want to kidnap me? Mas asked himself. That idea was as preposterous as trying to figure out who was behind Haruo's disappearance. Who even knew Mas or cared enough to take him? It wasn't like those masked men at Sonya de Groot's house knew who he was. But he had given out his Oriental Gardening business card with his home address to somebody recently, hadn't he? His business card, in fact, was one of the few places that advertised his full name (over the past five years, he might have given out three cards). Mas then remembered — the Hina House doll dealer down in San Diego. That fellow, Les Klinger, had indeed seemed like a *henna otoko,* strange man who lived in his own world. Was it possible that he had passed along Mas's information to someone like Estacio Pena? Or perhaps Haruo had gone to Hina House directly to resell the stolen *hina* dolls back to them?

Mas sped down the 5 like his truck was on fire. It was almost as if a supernatural force was protecting him as he passed Highway Patrol car after Highway Patrol car apprehending speeders. The Ford in their eyes was perhaps not worth ticketing. Anonymity was all that Mas and the Ford had going for them, and they would embrace it for all it was worth.

When he reached Hina House, Mas attempted to find the screwdriver on the floor of the passenger side, only to feel the sharp edges of keys and then the rough vinyl of a wallet. The Buckwheat Beauty had forgotten her valuables, but then there probably was no need for them in group. Mas stuck the keys and wallet in his front left pocket and his screwdriver in his right.

He pressed the doorbell, forgetting that it would unleash the "Sakura" cherry blossom song. *Ding-ding-DONG, ding-ding-DONG,* it rang like the bells of a Buddhist priest dur-

244

ing a memorial service. Mas put his ear to the door. Was that the soft crunch of footsteps and then pressure against the other side of the door as if someone was peering through the peephole?

Mas rang the doorbell again — *ding-ding-DONG, ding-ding-DONG* — and again and again. He swore that he would not move in spite of how anxious the noisy doorbell was making him feel. He would keep ringing until he busted the bell and after that he planned to move on to banging the door.

Finally the doorknob turned and Les Klinger appeared, his arm in a sling. "I took a fall recently," he explained. "It takes me awhile to get around now."

Mas charged past the doll man and the eerie blow-up dolls floating in the swimming pool and entered the darkened showroom. The hairs on his arms prickled — did he hear soft murmuring from the dolls in the different corners of the room? Was it the wooden *kokeshi,* straight-as-a-nail erect backs and rice-bowl haircuts, clattering by the floor? The melodious chanting of the *hina* dolls cascading down the wall, the drums gently beating? Or perhaps the Friendship Doll, Miss Tsuneo, crying in her glass prison?

Was there a secret door somewhere? Was

Haruo locked up in a spare bedroom?

"Wherezu Haruo? Wherezu my friend?" Mas whipped around, and the display lights seemed to swirl in circles like cosmic stars. "Was my friend here?"

"I don't know what or who you are talking about." Klinger, cradling his wrist, looked confused. His *mukuchi* wife, the woman without a mouth, stood beside him.

Mas was tired of all the lies and deception. The problem had started here. The *hina* dolls. Everyone wanted them, and someone had them and yet was not satisfied. Hina House knew their secrets.

"Who you tell dat I come here last week?" Mas yelled. His voice was as rough as frayed rope and its harshness surprised even him.

Klinger adjusted his glasses with his good hand. His wife's eyes were as big as billiard balls. "Nobody," he murmured.

"Whatsu special about those dolls?" What was their power, their black magic? Surely they were not as common as the doll man had described them. Because if they were, why were so many wanting them?

The doll man and his wife stood stunned, frozen. Mas needed answers and he didn't care whom he hurt at this point. Haruo's life was in danger; he could feel it in his bones. Maybe he was just a nobody gardener like Mas, but the Bomb had spared them both. Mas used to think that it had been a cruel joke, but in recent years, there seemed to be an additional purpose to their lives. That Haruo might be sacrificed for two dolls was no way to end his life.

Mas took another spin around the room, and his eyes followed the main spotlight on the queen of the castle, the Friendship Doll. As he made his way to Miss Tsuneo, Noriko, the wife, literally cringed behind her husband. Mas gripped the screwdriver like an ice pick and, turning his head away, he stabbed into the glass case. The protective box shattered into giant pieces, a broken shard slicing into the side of Mas's hand. Mas winced in pain but had to keep going. As loose broken pieces fell, tinkling against each other like wind chimes, he pulled out Miss Tsuneo and, using a professional wrestler's move, crushed her head in the crook of his arm as blood dripped down his hand into his sleeve.

"Be careful!" Les called out, and then his wife squeaked as if to add an extra exclamation mark.

"Izu want the truth," Mas said, swinging the doll back and forth. The doll was actually the size of a small child and Mas could not believe what he was doing.

"Watch the blood!" Klinger screamed.

Noriko's mouth was now wide open, revealing her square white teeth, shaped like a Christmas nutcracker's.

Mas felt like he was going to be sick. This couple actually thought of the doll as their child.

"You give my address to somebody."

"No, no, I said nothing about you." Sweat streamed down Klinger's forehead. "In fact, I almost forgot about you until today."

Again, Mas could have been offended, but this was no time for *hokori,* pride. "But you hidin' sumptin about those *hina* dolls."

Noriko squeaked again and Mas knew that he was on the right track.

"Yes, yes, I did a swap. An exchange."

Mas wiped some of the blood onto his five o'clock shadow. He could only imagine what a madman he must resemble.

"I knew that there was something different about these sets of dolls because of the interest we were receiving. The dolls historically are not that unusual — in fact, we have an exact set in storage.

"So I took the dolls apart, starting with the heads, and what do I find but a wire connected to some kind of audio-recording device set in the platform base. The recorder was old, a Minifon from the forties. The battery was dead, and even when I replaced it, the recorder didn't work. But sure enough there were two tiny reels and skinny audiotape. I knew what I had was some kind of spy device from around World War Two."

"Whatsu on the tape?"

The doll man's upper lip trembled. "I'm not sure. My plan was to listen to the tape before handing it over to the authorities. A Japanese man, an old man, came by a couple of days ago. He almost insinuated that I had made the swap of the dolls. How would he know? He hadn't even purchased the dolls."

Mas demanded the tape and the recorder, but the two remained unmoved. Upon shaking Miss Tsuneo a few times, Mas finally got the attention of the doll man.

"It's in the back bedroom." He stepped forward, but Mas gestured toward the wife instead.

"She," Mas said.

"Noriko, *ikkinasai*," Klinger directed his wife.

"No police," warned Mas.

"No police," Klinger repeated.

Noriko bowed slightly before disappearing into the hallway. She emerged in a few minutes, the tape and recorder resting in outstretched hands. The whole recorder was

no bigger than a half a sandwich, the reel
the size of a silver dollar. Could this be the
reason Chuck Blanco was killed and Haruo
kidnapped?

"Can I have her back now?" Klinger
asked, his arms outstretched toward the
doll, anticipating a big *dakko,* parent-child
embrace.

"One more thing." While still clutching
Miss Tsuneo's head, Mas pulled Spoon's
wallet from his left pocket and shoved a
photo in front of Klinger's face. "Dat
Japanese man who came ova, itsu him?"

Klinger lifted up his glasses, narrowed his
eyes, and then nodded. "Yes, that's him."

CHAPTER THIRTEEN

Once they were buried or burned, dead people, Mas imagined, didn't have any sort of ethnic identity. They didn't know that they were Mexican, Chinese, or Japanese, but the relatives they left behind did. That's why a place like Lopez, Sing, and Iwasaki Mortuary was born in the heart of Los Angeles's Lincoln Heights, just across from Plaza de la Raza, where young Latinos cut out skeletal images from bright colored tissue paper at Day of the Dead workshops every October.

Although he had experienced some rough patches in the 1980s, Itchy Iwasaki was making a tidy sum in his mortuary partnership, especially because he was in charge of the Japanese bereavements. Funerals were big deals in this ethnic community — you could see from the paid obituaries in the *Los Angeles Times.* At least one and sometimes even up to three — what a bonanza!

— of the approximately twenty obits were topped with a Japanese name. And more often than not, if it was a man's name, an image of an American flag accompanied it, a testament to those who had fought in either World War Two, Korea, or Vietnam.

Of course, it didn't mean one out of twenty people in Southern California was Japanese. The reality was much, much less. But if you judged from the hoopla in the obituary section, you would come to a very different conclusion.

Mas had initially thought that Itchy, who joined the mortuary in the eighties, had been related to Spoon, but now he was convinced that the connection was on Ike's side. It had been hard for Itchy to establish himself in the field, with so many competing mortuaries southwest of Lincoln Heights in Little Tokyo. It had required Itchy to take some desperate measures — maybe not so harmful, but perhaps not so ethical, either.

So Mas pounded up the stairs to Itchy's office, in search of two dead men. After he received his answer, he knew what he would say to the widow in her home in Montebello.

Like the doll man, Spoon did not come to her door no matter how many times the doorbell rang. There was nothing musical about Spoon's bell — it seemed to administer an electric shock to the comatose house. Except for Sonya, sneaking looks through her drapes, there was literally no one at home on the cul-de-sac during the day, so Mas could be as *urusai,* noisy, as a blood-thirsty watchdog. Mas altered his tactics and began pounding the door with his good left fist. He had ripped the middle of his T-shirt and wrapped it around the cut on his right hand to stop the bleeding. The dried blood was brick red, already crusted like old paint over T-shirt rags.

Finally the doorknob began to turn, and it was Spoon, in her trademark off-white sweater. Keeping the chain on the door, she cringed to see the blood on the side of Mas's face and glanced beyond his silhouette, as if she were worried that someone else was on the porch. She closed the door, removed the chain lock, and reopened the door.

"Come in," she whispered.

Mas entered, then the door and the chain lock were resecured. Spoon offered no explanations and excuses for why she had first ignored Mas's ringing of the bell. And why she was being so cautious now. Didn't Haruo say that sometimes Spoon forgot to lock the front door at night?

"What happened to you?" she asked meekly. When Itchy had asked the same question, Mas lied and said it had been a tree-cutting accident.

This time he offered no explanation, only that he had come from Itchy's mortuary in Lincoln Heights.

Spoon nodded. "He called me." She sank on one end of the couch and hugged an embroidered pillow to her chest as if to cushion a blow. Mas noticed that the Girls' Day platform of stacked shoe boxes was gone. Spoon gestured for Mas to sit across from her on a love seat.

What had Itchy told her? When Mas had arrived at his office, the mortuary man seemed congenial at first, pulling at his sunburned earlobes as usual when he said hello. But when Mas mentioned Ike Hayakawa's name, it seemed harder for Itchy to keep up the sides of his smile.

"Itchy wanted to know how you found out," reported Spoon.

It had been a weird hunch. Maybe all this time Mas wondered about Itchy's good luck and his sudden cash infusion in the eighties. When you yourself didn't have much good fortune, you are brutally aware of another man's jackpot.

"You know what he did?"

Spoon shook her head. "Not until recently." Her face was the color of rice paste — she really looked unwell but not shocked. If Mas had discovered that a stranger's dead body had been substituted for his spouse's, he would not be so calm.

It hadn't been only a nagging suspicion about Itchy's launching of the mortuary partnership back in the eighties. That was tangential, actually, the piece that was helpful in tying up the loose ends. What was much more curious was that both Ike and Jorg had indicated to their children that they were expecting to die on the same day. They were just driving to Hanley, not flying to the Middle East on a combat mission. And then, what a coincidence, each had taken out a million-dollar life-insurance policy. Quite convenient to guarantee a strong future for both their families.

And then there were the dead bodies that had been found at the Hanley car crash. Blanco had said that they had most likely been doused with gasoline and set on fire. Mas knew enough about burned remains — you always went for the teeth. The teeth left a trail leading to their owner.

That's why before the Buckwheat Beauty got out of his truck at the residential facility, Mas had asked, "You papa gotsu dentures?"

"Yes," she said, "he got all his teeth extracted when he was still in his fifties. Too much candy, I guess. That's why he always told Uncle Jorg to go to the dentist, but Uncle Jorg didn't listen to him. Funny, such a big man afraid of the dentist."

So no teeth trail — Mas filed that information away. He then felt confident to charge into Lopez, Sing, and Iwasaki Mortuary and demand some answers.

Itchy instantly became jittery, his left thumb dancing against the papers on his desk.

"Okay, Ike came to me," Itchy finally admitted. "Said that he need two corpses. One about his size and one about six feet tall. I told him that he was crazy — I couldn't just hand over two of our clients' bodies. That would be against the law.

"But I had my connection with the coroner's office and they have a backlog of indigents, unclaimed bodies — whaddaya call it, potter's field. They are cremated, filed, and buried in a lot over there on the side of Evergreen Cemetery.

"So I told them that we were willing to take on the cremations as a service, even look after some of the burials. They were more than willing to work with us. Out of all those bodies, I found two that fit the profiles Ike gave me. I didn't know what he wanted with them. He said that he wouldn't be hurting people, that actually he would be saving lives. He told me to extract all the teeth from the shorter man before I prepared the bodies for him.

"They came here to pick up the bodies in huge athletic duffel bags. I didn't know what they were going to do with them. But those were dead bodies already. I didn't kill anyone and neither did they. Later, when I heard about Ike and Jorg dying, I didn't know what to think. I didn't want to get the business in trouble, so I kept quiet."

And kept the money Ike gave you, thought Mas. This Ike Hayakawa was a detail person, the type that made plans and actually followed them. He was a headman, a smart man who could move in different circles deftly and elegantly like a ballroom dancer. He wasn't like Mas, who didn't know how to water down or sweeten an insult or alter the way he spoke or walked into a room.

Mas stared directly at Spoon. "I know heezu alive," he said. She immediately lowered her eyes, which meant she knew it too.

The back bedroom door flew open and

Mas literally leaped out of his seat.

The figure in the doorway walked closer to the light. The same thick hair in the photographs, only now it was all silver gray. The aviator glasses had been replaced by rectangular plastic-framed tinted ones that artists and actors wear. Instead of a short-sleeved button-down shirt, he had on a baby blue velour sweatsuit, the uniform of suburban wannabe rappers.

Mas had only one question for the dead man, Ike Hayakawa. "Whatchu do wiz Haruo?"

The dead man wanted to start from the beginning, so Mas let him. Minutes and hours were ticking away, but he claimed that he knew nothing about Haruo Mukai, other than Haruo was going to marry his wife. He sat on the couch next to Spoon, nursing a fizzy drink and a lit cigarette.

"Occupational hazard," he explained. "I had quit a while back and now everyone around me is smoking."

Mas surprisingly didn't crave the tobacco smell at that moment. His stomach was completely *kara,* empty, and the only way it could be sated was by explanations. He couldn't help noticing how comfortable Ike was in his former home. How long had he been there? Ever since Spoon had kicked out Dee, Mas imagined.

"My family started off growing pompons in Montebello. You know what they are?"

Mas nodded. He was familiar with the fat chrysanthemums that the Japanese used to grow. They were sometimes as large as cabbage, their stems bent from all the weight they carried.

"My family was one of the early ones that came before the alien land laws. We were able to actually buy land. Can you believe it? We built a greenhouse, an actual one with pane glass, not those temporary fixtures with cheesecloth muslin."

The Hayakawas were among the elite, that was for sure. They didn't have to wander throughout the desolate desert every season, following truck farmers. They didn't have to carry blankets for their heads to sleep in shacks. The Hayakawas owned land, so they could stay put, build a house, go to the same school for several years, be smart.

"My father was the one who was close to Mr. de Groot. The de Groots first belonged to the other side of the market, the European side. But we both farmed in Montebello, and Jorg and me, we grew up together. A group of these Nisei boys were giving Jorg a hard time, being so big, you know, and quiet. So I spoke out. My mother told me that my words could cut like a knife. Didn't have to beat on anyone, make physical threats.

"My dad died right before World War Two, so I guess I was the man in charge. The de Groots offered to take care of the farm, didn't know what we would do if it hadn't been for them. We got married in camp —" Ike paused and grinned at Spoon, who had been tearing at her dead cuticles the whole time of his monologue. "And then just when the conflict overseas was ending I got drafted, can you believe it? Was part of the Counter Intelligence Corps and spent some time in Japan. We helped interrogate prisoners of war, were a watchdog for communism."

"Spy," Mas couldn't help but murmur and Ike nodded.

"I guess we were. Counter intelligence officer sounds a lot better."

"*Hina.* Those *hina* dolls come from Japan. Spy dolls."

Ike nodded again. "It was a pet project of one of the other officers. He didn't want to bring them back to the States so I asked him if I could. We just used them as regular Girls' Days dolls, and you know what, I completely forgot about them having a recording device. That is, until Dee started getting into trouble." Ike's voice became thin and fragile, quite a contrast to the relaxed, friendly way he had started the conversation. His drink had melted and his cigarette was long extinguished.

"Whatsu on tape?" Mas brought the conversation back to what was in his pocket.

Ike looked up sharply and Mas immediately realized that he had shown his hand too early. "You know where it is? Who has it?"

"Dat doll man in San Diego."

"I knew that he was hiding something. He switched the dolls, didn't he?" Ike got up quickly before Mas could stop him. The tape felt like it was on fire in his pocket and his hand instinctively went to his thigh to protect it.

Ike remained as still as a statue, and as he slowly bent down into the couch, his knees cracked. His pupils seemed to expand like a rabid dog's.

"I need that tape," he said plainly.

"I wanna know whatsu on it. You know dat Chuck Blanco's dead."

Ike didn't seem surprised. "You don't need to know anything. It'll be safer for you and safer for Spoon."

"Give him the tape, Mas," Spoon said

softly. She wasn't pleading or begging. More like a warning.

Mas balled up his fists, grimacing as pain surged from his cut hand. He stood up. "No, you tell me first — whatsu on dat tape? My friend's gone and I needsu to know."

"It's Estacio Pena's confession."

Mas frowned. Confession about what? That he was selling drugs out in Imperial Valley? Mas didn't know much about American drug laws, but that had taken place close to twenty years ago. Hadn't too much time elapsed to get him now?

"Confession that he was never going to get prosecuted for his crimes. The DEA was out to get him. Well, more than him, his father. His father ran a drug cartel that bled into California and Arizona. The weak link: Estacio Pena, the bastard son. So when Dee was arrested, the DEA approached me. They needed my help, some way to convince Dee to give Estacio up. But she told everyone that she knew nothing. She was telling the truth, but that wasn't going to help her case. So I told the DEA that I'd help them, that I'd contact Estacio Pena and tell him that I'd be willing to smuggle in some drugs — as long as he left Dee alone.

"So I tracked him down. He came to the

house and the dolls were ready for him — just my own security plan, you have to understand. Jorg helped me through the whole thing. But as we were talking, Estacio kept bragging that he was protected, that his father had the government in his back pocket. He kept mentioning the CIA. That the CIA was looking out for his father because he was one of the rebel leaders who were going to take the Nicaraguan government down.

"I thought that Estacio was bluffing, just tooting his horn as usual. But the deeper and deeper Jorg and I got into it, nothing was happening to Estacio. We didn't make one drug run — we made seven. We gave all the information to the DEA, but somehow Estacio was always elusive. He was one step ahead of the authorities, always.

"It was the Hanley police. Practically all were on the take. Everyone except for Chuck Blanco. He was the only honest cop on the force. Too bad he wasn't that smart. I'm sorry that he's dead.

"We told the DEA that we wanted out of this undercover business, but they wouldn't let us. Said that they had enough on us to prosecute us — but for what? It was their deal, after all. They weren't going to help us, so Jorg and I decided that we needed to take drastic steps."

"You fake the car accident."

Ike nodded. "We didn't know what else to do. Estacio's men kept warning us that if anything happened to Pena's son, our families would be killed. For me, it made sense to sacrifice my identity — Dee was my daughter. But Jorg —" Ike's voice cracked. "He didn't have to do any of it. He just did it because he was my friend."

What happened to them afterward, Mas wondered. How could one live a life incognito after having a wife and raising a family?

"Now, I'll need that tape." Ike tugged at the waist of his sweatpants and brought out a gun. It was black and had a long attachment on its barrel.

Mas did have a little experience with guns, enough to know that Ike wasn't playing around.

"Put that away," admonished Spoon. "That's not necessary. Mas will give up that tape without any rough stuff."

Mas removed the reel from his pocket. The ends of the brown audiotape were thin and tangled, but the meat of the recording was intact.

Ike grabbed the tape. This was the prize he had been searching for during the past week. For what? Blackmail? To ruin Estacio's father's political career? Or perhaps as a carrot to snag a very big and bad rabbit.

The doorbell rang.

The three of them stayed frozen in between the couch and the love seat. Who could that be?

"Spoon, see who it is."

Spoon pulled out a plastic footstool underneath a table and looked through the peephole.

"It's Dee."

Mas got on his knees and angled his head so that he could spy through a decorative side window covered with an opaque curtain. *"Matte!"* He whispered for them to wait before taking action. "Someone wiz her."

Ike hunched over next to Mas. "Estacio." The old man moved toward the hallway as gracefully as a cat. "I'll be back here. Let them in."

Keeping the door chained, Spoon slowly turned the knob. Seizing his opportunity, Estacio pressed Dee face's into the crack of the open door, revealing the presence of a gun. "Let us in, Mrs. Hayakawa," he hissed, "or I'll shoot your daughter right on this welcome mat."

Spoon's hands shook as she struggled to undo the chain. As soon as the door was freed, Estacio pushed Dee into the house and slammed the door shut behind them.

"I'm sorry, Mom." Dee fell into her mother's arms while Estacio aimed his gun at Mas's head.

"So where is it?"

Mas felt that he was in a movie. Surely, this could not be happening to him, the Buckwheat Beauty, and Haruo's fiancée in the middle of Montebello.

"I know that you have it, old man. Klinger told my man — at least while he was alive."

"Dunno whatchu talkin' about."

Estacio grabbed Dee by the elbow and pushed her down to her knees, the gun aimed at her head.

"Old lady, come here," he ordered Spoon. She knelt next to her daughter and reached for her hand.

"Both of you, put your hands on your head." Their backs toward Mas, the mother and daughter unclasped hands and com-piled.

"I'm sorry, Mom, I'm sorry for every-thing."

"Shut up, Dee," Estacio ordered and aimed the gun barrel toward Spoon's head. "So, old man, it's all up to you. The longer you wait before telling me the truth, I kill one of them. First the the old lady. And then Dee."

Mas bit down on his lip. Wasn't the dead man supposed to intervene at some point?

"So what's it going to be?"

Estacio turned toward Mas in frustration, and his eyes widened as if he had seen a ghost. "Shit," he murmured and then the *whoosh-clack* sound resembling the release of a staple gun and the smell of smoke. Estacio's head slammed against the china cabinet, spraying a red halo of blood on the mint green wall, before slumping to the carpeted floor.

Dee screamed and covered her face. Seeking to console her daughter, Spoon wrapped her in her oversized sweater.

Mas looked back at the hallway, only to see right into the back bedroom. The window over the bed had been slid wide open, its screen thrown onto the floor. The curtains blew in from a spring breeze, a perfect scene of domesticity, belying the violence that had just occurred a room away.

Officers Chang and Gallegos came on the scene within a matter of minutes. They had received an anonymous call about trouble brewing inside the Hayakawa house. Ike had definitely come through on that.

They came in with their guns cocked and ready. They stepped around the pool of blood underneath Estacio's body, the hole in his head releasing a busted persimmon of brains.

"Who shot this man?" Officer Gallegos asked.

"I don't know." Dee spoke first and then her mother.

Mas shook his head too. He didn't feel that any of them were lying. Spoon perhaps had known him at one time. Maybe Dee did as well. But the dead man who had returned home was indeed a stranger. His world had changed and so had he.

CHAPTER FOURTEEN

The police officers must have thought it best to get to the truth by dividing and conquering. They split up Mas, Spoon, and the Buckwheat Beauty in separate rooms and even the backyard to question them. Officer Chang picked Mas.

"What happened to your hand?"

Mas had forgotten all about the incident at Hina House. Was the doll man dead as Estacio had boasted? "Tree cuttin' accident," he said.

They sat in the bedroom that the Buckwheat Beauty was using. It had a futon on the hardwood floor and a guitar in the corner. Mas remembered that Dee said that she was into music — in fact, that was how Estacio "Steve" Pena came into her life.

"Tell me what happened, Mr. Arai."

Mas wasn't sure what he was going to say, but he knew that there was no mentioning the dead man. Other than that fact, he basically reported the truth: that he had come to talk to Spoon about her missing fiancé, his best friend. And that Dee had come to the door with a gun pointed at her head.

"Did you know the assailant?"

Mas shook his head vigorously. No, he did not.

"Who else was in the house with you?"

"Spoon."

"Mrs. Hayakawa?"

Mas nodded.

"And who else?"

"Dee."

"And?"

"I dunno."

"Then who shot Mr. Pena?"

Mas shrugged his shoulders. "I hear gun, look back, and bedroom door and window wide open."

"Seems like you would have heard someone go through the bedroom window while you were in the house."

"My hearing, not so good, *yo*," Mas said. "I ole man, you knowsu."

Officer Chang tried to suppress a smile, but the corners of her mouth tugged up in spite of herself. She composed herself to look more serious and suspicious. "We're having that entire room dusted for prints, so I hope for all of your sakes that we have

270

evidence that indeed another person was in that room."

After the interrogation by the uniformed officers, Mas, Spoon, and Dee were all told that they would have to go to the police station later to speak to detectives. And they would all have to spend the night somewhere else as the house would be further examined for evidence. Already yellow tape was stretched across the living room and Mas held back an inclination to gag as he saw the bloodstains splattered on a bookcase and parts of the mint green walls.

Spoon's eldest daughter Debra had arrived to take the two women to her house, but Spoon waved her off. "You take Dee. I need to talk to Mas alone, so I'll have him drive me."

The Buckwheat Beauty gave Mas a quick hug before getting into her sister's minivan. "I didn't say a word," she whispered in his ear. "And I won't say anything, either."

Mas backed away from the girl. What was she saying? That Mas had been the gunman? That didn't make any sense. Because first of all, if Mas had had a real gun in his hands, he would have ended up shooting holes in the ceiling and the wall, rather than getting the side of Estacio's head in one try. And second, where was the murder weapon?

271

That kept the authorities scratching their heads. Because if it indeed had been Mas, Spoon, or Dee, where was the gun?

Mas didn't bother to refute Dee's contention. With police officers — both uniformed and in plain clothes — wandering in and out of the Montebello house, this wasn't the time to make any private pronouncements. If it gave the Buckwheat Beauty some comfort that an older man was looking after her, then so be it. It was actually true, just that Mas had not been the one.

After watching her two daughters disappear down the street in the candy-apple-red van, Spoon lingered in front of the wood-framed house across the street. The de Groot property now had a FOR SALE sign on its yellowing lawn.

There was still a spray of Estacio's blood on Spoon's salt-and-pepper hair and her sweater, but Mas didn't bother to bring it up. He was sure that Spoon would hit the showers the minute she arrived at Debra's house. And the sweater would be burned or thrown away. There was no need for any reminders of what happened today.

"Everything's changing," she muttered.

Actually, everything had changed years ago, but nobody wanted to admit it at the time. Now, with blood on their hair, face, and clothing, there was no denying it.

"I thought I was losing my mind, Mas," Spoon said when they were traveling to Monterey Park. Mas thought she was talking about the gun being aimed at her head, but actually she was talking about when she first laid eyes on the resurrected Ike. "I had been sleeping on the couch and then I heard something. I look and there he is, going out the door with the *hina* dolls."

She pressed her fingers on her closed eyelids, as if to replay the scene in her mind. "He turned back for a second, a split second, and sees me see him. He doesn't say a word, but his eyes — I'd recognize those eyes anywhere even with those silly glasses.

"I didn't sleep one bit that night. I didn't know what to think. Dee gets up and then starts screaming about the missing dolls. What can I tell her, that her dead father went off with them? I know that I can't get married that day. Either I'm hallucinating or my husband is still alive.

"So I call off the wedding, hoping that I'd figure it out in a couple of days. But then Dee starts making a bigger fuss about the dolls, even calling the police. I had to go along with it, at least for a little while.

"Then a couple of days later, he shows

up. Ike. I'm alone in the house and he's on my back doorstep. I practically faint, right then and there. He wants to know if I had done anything with the dolls. Nothing, nothing. I spent three thousand on them because they were a symbol of what we once were. But I don't really care about the dolls. I want to know why my husband is alive twenty years after he was supposed to have burned in a car accident.

"He says that he will tell me everything after he finds those dolls, his dolls. He goes to Hina House, but they seem not to know anything. I mean, why should they lie? So he figures that it's the government or other authorities who have taken the tape. Either way, he wants to get Estacio Pena. Kill him. Extinguish his life. So even if he doesn't have the tape, he pretends that he does. He calls him anonymously. Threatens him that he has evidence that will shame his father. Destroy his political reputation and his relationship with the U.S. government."

Mas could not understand the passion of this man, his commitment to do someone in after so many years. Perhaps it was because Ike had achieved the American dream, held it in his hands, seen it secured by friends even when the government was after him. It must have been a bitter blow to have this dream crumble — not from the outside, but from the inside, from his precious youngest daughter.

"Ike blamed himself. He really did. He worked so hard but at the expense of the girls, especially Dee. She has a different kind of personality than the two older girls. More sensitive. More emotionally needy. Debra and Donna are more like Ike and me. Task oriented. We like to get things done. But Dee, as the youngest, always felt ignored, neglected. We were all so busy with the business; we didn't really spend time with each other as a family."

Spoon told of her counseling sessions with Dee and Ike. "It finally occurred to him that all work and money were meaningless. All of the achievements didn't mean lickety-squat. That was a huge revelation, you know. That what you've been striving for all these years wasn't worth that much."

It sure smelled like Spoon was giving her husband an easy way out. "He fake dat heezu dead. Dat *orai* wiz you?"

"Of course not. All the pain that he caused me and the girls, especially Dee? And not to mention Jorg and Sonya. And Geoff. I can't bear to even think of them. Why would Jorg be so foolish to take on this horrible responsibility?"

Jorg the Dutchman. Where was he, anyway? Ike had not mentioned his friend's current whereabouts. And the way Spoon was talking about him, Mas figured that he was dead.

"He adored Ike. Saw him like a brother he never had. It probably hurt him to see Ike in so much anguish. He probably wasn't thinking when he went on those first drug runs with Ike. And then it was too late.

"Do you know that Estacio threatened Jorg? Said that his men would kill Sonya and Geoff if anything happened to him? At that point, Ike and Jorg thought for the sake of us, their families, they needed to disappear, die.

"That's why, Mas, you cannot say anything to Dee or the other two girls. Or to Sonya. They made this sacrifice so that we'd be safe. And we have to accept it or else all of this was for nothing."

Spoon explained that even Casey had a role in the deception. "Do you know that he thought Ike was really a drug runner? He even attempted to blackmail Geoff after his father had died. That didn't work, so he tried to take over the route in Hanley himself. It didn't take, I guess. But Geoff never forgot and never forgave."

Mas wondered if Spoon had shared this

with the dead man. Being locked up in the same house for a few days was the perfect environment to unload a lifetime of secrets.

"You need to forget everything that happened today." Spoon began rocking back and forth in the passenger seat. "And I'm not doing this just to protect Ike. Far from it. This Ike isn't the same man I married. In fact, we were having a lot of marital problems back then."

Mas remembered Sonya's stories of Ike moving in with them during some rough patches in the Hayakawa union.

"Ike was always so restless. He wanted new challenges to conquer. He wanted to sell the business and start another one, run off to Hawaii or some other exotic place. 'What about the children?' I asked. 'They're all grown up,' he said. And then Dee got into trouble, a reminder that what he started was unfinished, maybe even not done right."

Spoon finally stopped moving in her seat. "These past few days when I was sequestered in the house with Ike, do you know what I was thinking?"

Mas shook his head.

"That I missed Haruo." Her sad eyes met Mas's. "I felt so guilty because Dee was accusing him of stealing the dolls. And I said nothing, except for reporting that I paid only a few hundred dollars for them. Just a minor theft, nothing big." She covered her face again. "I know that's a poor excuse. I have to tell him that I'm sorry. You have to find him."

What do you think I've been doing these past five days? Mas thought. In the beginning, he had been the only one sounding the alarm. Now that the mystery of the dolls had been solved, people were finally moving on to the true innocent, Haruo.

"Whaddabout your husband?" Mas didn't want to be *hinikui,* twisting the truth into her gut, but this new discovery could not be ignored.

"That man is not my husband," Spoon said. "My husband has been dead for twenty years."

When Mas got home, he called G.I. and Juanita and filled them in on the news.

"Unbelievable," Juanita said.

"Yeah, sounds like you were in some kind of assassin movie," G.I. said from the second line. "Pretty soon they'll be calling you Mas the Badass."

Juanita started laughing, and for a second, Mas contemplated hanging up the phone. He'd gone through too much that day to suffer any ridicule. Juanita regained her composure. "Get off the phone, G.I. I have to talk to Mas about business," she said.

"No offense, Mas. I'll be talking to you."

The click of the second line and then Juanita reported what she had discovered about the postcard from Phoenix. "That particular postcard is provided to certain resorts and hotels, more on the high-end side. My girlfriend knew someone at the company that distributes them and when I mentioned the strange message, the sales rep got a bit cagey.

"In other words, she knew exactly what I was talking about. Turns out she had Homeland Security calling her because someone was sending these postcards with strange messages to all these government offices. Not necessarily threatening messages, but accusing the CIA of wrongdoing. Finally, she told me which one of her customers — a retirement resort in Phoenix.

"I called the activities director, and after I told her the postcard story, she says, 'Oh, that's Richard Mars.' He was apparently suffering from Alzheimer's, got really bad last year. The activities director scanned his ID photo and e-mailed it to me. He was of Dutch descent, she explained, loved all the Dutch pastries, so they were monitoring his diet.

"I remembered what you told me about Ike Hayakawa's good friend, Jorg de Groot. That his heritage was from Holland. Found an old photo on a news story about the accident. It was the same guy, Mas. Only twenty years older. This Richard Mars is definitely Jorg de Groot."

"So Jorg de Groot is alive?"

"Well, actually he died last year. Natural causes in the retirement home. And unfortunately alone."

After hearing about Jorg de Groot, Mas couldn't fall asleep for a while. What had Jorg de Groot been doing for the past twenty years? He had gone incognito, underground for the sake of his friend. Mas wasn't sure that he would do that for anyone, even Haruo, but somehow knew Haruo would do that for him.

Mas finally willed himself to sleep and when he did, he became Urashima Taro in his dreams. There, he saved a turtle from some bullying boys and was invited to spend time in the Turtle World. They were under the sea, prancing and dancing, feeling the security of warm water protecting them from the harshness of dry land life. But then Mas was washed ashore, and as he walked barefoot through downtown Los Angeles and finally Altadena, nothing was familiar. The grand old buildings in Pasadena had been replaced by high-rises and his wood-framed house was gone; in fact, his own street had been plowed over. The houses had been replaced by piles of rocks, smooth and flat like the ones currently in Genessee Howard's backyard.

At around five o'clock, his phone rang. Maybe three hours of sleep at best?

"Mas." Taxie's voice, which had recently taken on a hard, clipped tone, reminding Mas of stale rice crackers. "They are requesting that you come into the market for a special meeting. Noon."

Mas agreed. After Taxie clicked off, Mas realized that he hadn't asked, "Who's they?" or "What kind of special meeting?"

The rest of the morning consisted of Yuban coffee. A couple of games of solitaire. And then Mas finally picked up the phone and pressed a long string of numbers. A very familiar answering machine. Mas was going to hang up but forced himself to stay on and leave a message.

"Hallo," he said, "itsu Dad."

As Mas approached the market, he saw a familiar figure on the southwest corner of Wall and Seventh. The giant black man with the bean sprout–shaped head and body. Mas pulled to the red-painted curb and, turning off the engine, slid over to the passenger side of the banana-yellow seat and rolled the window halfway down because that was as far as it would go.

"Hey, I see you talkin' to Roberto yesterday," Mas said.

The man frowned. "Roberto. I know probably ten Robertos."

"This one from the flower market."

"The only person that I really knew at the market was Casey. The nicest guy. Dropped off old bread from the flower market bakery once a week to us in Skid Row. And took us to the racetrack all the time."

"You got money to gamble?"

"It was fun because we always won. Casey gave us the winning ticket to trade in. All we had to do was sign for it with an address and fake social security number. We'd get five bucks a ticket for our trouble. It was nice to be a winner for once. Even though it really only lasted a few minutes."

Mas traced the lip of his Clippers mug attached to his dashboard. What had Casey been up to? He thanked the man for the information and pulled a five-dollar bill from his pocket. He could not offer the man the fleeting experience of being a winner, but cash was still cash.

As he entered the market, he saw a series of signs printed out from a computer taped on the columns throughout the second floor. SPECIAL MEETING. UPSTAIRS CONFERENCE ROOM. MANDATORY FOR ALL TENANTS.

The conference room, as it turned out, was really an old storage area. Boxes of green foam oases for flower arrangements were stacked against one wall to make way for at least a hundred metal folding chairs. Only about a third of the chairs were filled — so much for mandatory.

In front of the small crowd was Roberto, only he looked nothing like the same Roberto. He was wearing a pinstriped suit, for one thing, with an official-looking ID card around his neck.

Mas remained in the doorway but had already been spotted by the speaker. "Mr. Arai, please join us."

A bit confused, Mas took a seat on the end of the row toward the back. Not only did Roberto look different, he sounded different as well.

"My name is Bob Sanchez and I'm an investigator with the IRS," the speaker announced to the crowd.

"The IRS?" someone said in back of Mas.

"I thought he was from El Salvador."

"Yeah, well, turns out he's actually from El Sereno," another replied, referring to a small Los Angeles community just southwest of South Pasadena, not far from Mas's neighborhood.

This crowd didn't appreciate being duped, and expressed their disapproval by folding their arms and looking away when this Bob Sanchez spoke.

"The IRS is committed to cracking down on all tax violations, and this year we have been targeting gambling winnings violations. You know that all gambling winnings are fully taxable and must be reported on your tax return. You cannot claim winnings that are not yours and receive a percentage of the winnings. That is like receiving someone's wages that are not yours so that person will not have to pay tax on the money. This is fraud and is fully prosecutable under law.

"Now, we are fully aware that there was a very organized operation here in which the homeless population and others were recruited to get around the paying of taxes. This is illegal. Let me state this again: This is illegal."

Mas finally grasped what Sanchez was saying. The IRS had caught wind of a scam being generated by someone connected to the market. And that person had to be Casey.

"With the recent discovery of a dead body in the market, we are very concerned that this scheme may have gang-related connections. So we implore any of you who might know something to come forward."

With the mention of "gang," the room buzzed with talk. Could Casey's racetrack scheme have larger implications? After the mandatory meeting had officially ended, most of the people quickly trickled out of the room. Mas attempted to leave too, but the IRS agent hooked him by tapping on his shoulder.

"I'm worried about your friend Haruo," Sanchez said. "I had confronted him and I believe that he was moving close to helping us. The day I spoke to him was the day that he disappeared."

"You tell police?"

"Yes, our departments are working together on this. I hope we find him very soon — alive, of course."

Mas stumbled out of the concrete room, feeling sick to his stomach. Haruo was apparently getting ready to snitch. Is that why he had been kidnapped? If he had been in cahoots with Casey, did that mean he experienced the same fate? Had he also been discarded in some back alley in Skid Row?

"Mas, still no Haruo, yes?" Felipe, the owner of the massive Rose Emporium, was getting on the escalator down to the sales floor. "Come, come to my stall and I give you some bread and free flowers."

Mas didn't know what those things had to do with making him feel any better, but he didn't have the energy to refuse. He followed the energetic rose wholesaler down the escalator to his stall.

"Haruo's children are very concerned. To offer a ten-thousand-dollar reward, that is impressive." Felipe checked the moisture in one of his flower displays.

"Hontō?" Mas first responded in Japanese and then quickly corrected himself. "Really?"

"Mas, you haven't been reading your *Rafu,* have you?" Taxie waved a copy of Los Angeles's Japanese American daily newspaper from the next stall. "It even made it in the *Times.*"

Taxie, in fact, had a whole stack of newspapers featuring Haruo's scarred face on his worktable. How appropriate that his mug shot would be used to wrap cut flowers.

Felipe was about to grab a couple of long French baguettes next to his cash register when he got sidetracked by a noise from the back. "Oh, those cats, how did they get in here again? Making so much noise this week."

Mas narrowed his eyes. They were the same alley cats that were regulars in the parking lot.

"Whatsu ova there?" Mas gestured toward a door about three feet high next to the Rose Emporium stall.

"Oh, that's the dungeon. It's just storage for the market. Why do you ask?"

Mas ran toward the elf door, his movements scattering the two cats behind plastic containers filled with flowers.

"Somebody, open dis door."

"What's wrong, Mas?" Taxie walked out of his stall.

"Haruo, Haruo, you in there?" Mas placed his ear to the door. Was it his imagination or did he hear something?

Pico shot through the crowd and returned with a set of keys on a large metal ring.

"*Hayaku, hayaku.*" Hurry, hurry. Didn't matter if Pico didn't understand the words. He certainly understood Mas's tone.

The door creaked open, and the light, a bare bulb covered in spiderwebs, was snapped on. On his side lay Haruo Mukai, his hands and feet bound with duct tape. The miniroom smelled like urine, but who cared about a little *shi-shi* at a time like this? Most of his mouth had been taped too, except for one open corner that allowed for a large straw from a supersized 7-Eleven drink. Haruo's eyes were closed, his eyelashes caked with dried mucus.

"Haruo, Haruo." Mas struggled to tear the tape from his friend's mouth while Pico worked on the hands. A scab was left on a small bald spot on the front of his head. His lips were completely dehydrated, skin flaking off like the whites of a freshly peeled orange.

Slowly Haruo's good eye opened. "Mas." His voice was faint yet still audible. "Took you long enough."

Casey had told Haruo that he was just locking him up for a couple of days. "I'll call Taxie on Friday," he told him. "Just need the extra time to get out of L.A."

Haruo had promised that he wouldn't tell a soul. He wouldn't breathe a word about how Casey had taken him and two other homeless men to the track two times a week to claim winnings that weren't theirs. But Casey didn't believe him. He pulled Haruo by his hair, dragged him into the back of a van, bound Haruo's legs and hands, and finally delivered him into the tomb of the empty market.

"Casey knew that I couldn't do the cheatin' no more," he said to Mas as they waited for the paramedics.

"No *shinpai*, Haruo." Do not worry. No sense confessing when you were half dead. Someone had laid down a tarp onto the cold cement floor and Mas, Taxie, Pico, and Felipe had lifted Haruo out of the dungeon into the bright lights of the market.

"Haruo!"

Mas at first didn't recognize Spoon because she was wearing a bright orange cardigan and her hair was cropped short. She pushed her way through the men to get to Haruo's prostrate body.

"Youzu glad to see me?" Haruo asked.

Spoon didn't answer but hid her face in his bony chest. "When you're all better, we're getting married, first thing."

Haruo grinned, his dried-out lips bursting at the seams. "Izu gotta be kidnapped more often."

Haruo was taken to St. Vincent's Hospital, just west of downtown L.A. He was in the Japanese wing, which served sticky rice to anyone interested, Japanese or non-Japanese. Only family was allowed in his room, which meant Clement, Kiyomi and her husband, and even Spoon. But not Mas.

Mas was taking out his screwdriver on his walk back to the Ford when he noticed a figure smoking underneath one of the lampposts in the hospital parking lot.

"Your friend's doing all right?" the dead man asked.

"Weak from no food, five days. But heezu gotsu soda at least. Casey no want to kill him. But youzu almost did."

"I didn't touch the man."

"But you kill Casey."

Ike looked shocked. "I've always thought that I was an excellent judge of character. In fact, my superiors have been impressed by my uncanny intuition. But I must say that I underestimated you, Mas. You're definitely smarter than you look. Even the police believe that Estacio Pena killed Casey for a past deal gone wrong."

Ike was letting Estacio take the fall for Casey's execution. In light of all the trouble Estacio had caused, Mas shouldn't have cared. But each man should answer for his own crime, Mas believed.

"I'm leaving the country, so I thought I'd check in with you one time."

"Japan?" Mas asked.

"South of the border, that's my home now. That's where my wife lives. And our two sons."

Mas's eyes grew big. Spoon's husband was *toshiyori,* as old as Mas and Haruo — no, even older — but he was still *iki-iki,* energetic and virile enough to start a second family. Maybe living undercover did that for a man.

"I didn't tell Spoon. I didn't have to. She's a smart woman; you can't pull any fast ones on her." Ike adjusted his tinted glasses. "I just don't want Dee to know. Not any of it. She'll think that she caused all of it."

But she had, hadn't she?

"The truth is that I'm addicted to taking on different identities. If I had to be Ike Hayakawa my whole life —"

"Youzu the Chinito."

"I guess that's what they're calling me now. I'm getting way too old for any of this. I plan to get out of this undercover business next year." The dead man dropped his cigarette onto the concrete parking lot. "The thing I regret the most is dragging Jorg into all of this. Lying and pretending wasn't his kind of thing. He wasn't suited for this type of life. It must have been the stress, because he started forgetting things, or repeating the same thing over and over. I

291

got him to a doctor — early-onset Alzheimer's. I got him into the best facility in Phoenix — at least it was warm — and even saw him from time to time. He kept telling me that we'd be safe because the *hina* dolls held our secrets. And yes, he called them *hina*. Even though he didn't say too much, he had a facility for languages. Anyway, he told me that if Estacio Pena dared to do anything to our families, he'd expose him, his father, and the government. I asked him continuously where the dolls were, but he wouldn't tell me. 'You're not the only one with secrets,' he told me. He thought that he was being funny. Jorg had his own sly humor."

What would be happening with the audio evidence that had been hidden in the *hina* dolls for the past twenty years? Mas didn't have to ask his question out loud, because Ike eventually revealed the answer on his own.

"We're getting the taped confession to both governments — U.S. and Nicaragua — as well as some sympathetic media and web outlets. Maybe nobody will be arrested, but their reputations will be damaged. Estacio's father will be mourning not only his son's death but perhaps his political career."

How about the fingerprints of the dead

man all over the Montebello house?

Ike chuckled. "You'd be surprised how quickly that investigation will be snuffed out. Estacio Pena's death will be an unsolved mystery, thanks to my employer. My fingerprints are not on file on any governmental record.

"Look after Spoon and my girls, will you, Mas? Especially Dee. She needs some kind of father figure in her life."

I already got a daughter, Mas was thinking. *I don't want to take on one more.* But Ike needed some kind of reassurance, grease that would allow him to slip from his old life. So Mas nodded. He didn't feel like he was making a bald-faced *uso.* Haruo would be the new husband and stepfather now, and he was the best man for the job.

CHAPTER FIFTEEN

Kimono o kikaete obishimete
Kyowa watashimo hare sugata
Haru no yayoino konoyokihi
Naniyori ureshii Hina Matsuri

Changing into kimono, tightening the sash
Today I too look beautiful
For this special spring day
The happiest Hina Matsuri
— "Hina Matsuri Song," fourth stanza

After Haruo's kidnapping, his children purchased him a cell phone. "We want to know where you are at all times," said Kimiyi. Clement sat down with him and explained all the features — from answering to calling, taking pictures (especially handy during automobile accidents), and even playing games with cascading cubes. Days and weeks were spent mastering that phone, the size of a pocket calculator. Now Haruo was using the cell phone to call Mas every hour.

"Nanda!" Mas practically spat his exasperation onto his receiver as he answered his bedroom phone on its first ring.

"Dad, it's me. Is something wrong?"

"No, Haruo just goin' *kuru-kuru-pa.*"

"Oh, he's getting married tomorrow, right? You have to tell him congratulations from us."

Mari was like a second daughter to Haruo. But her giant *hakujin* husband Lloyd and their son Takeo? They were strangers. Mas didn't know if *omedetō* from the entire Jensen family would really mean anything to his friend.

"I know being the best man and all, you must be really busy," said Mari. There was something in the tone of her voice that sounded funny, almost too formal. Mas braced himself for an unexpected turn of events. He didn't have to wait long. "I wanted to tell you as soon as we decided. Dad, Lloyd's been offered a job in L.A. You won't believe it, but it's with Dodger Stadium. We're going to be moving to California."

For the next few minutes, Mas heard only blobs of noise, floating words encased in membrane, not having any particular contextual meaning. He was too shocked to even pursue what work Lloyd, the giant gardener, would be doing with his beloved baseball team. All Mas comprehended was that his only daughter and his grandson were going to be not only in same side of the country as he was, but maybe in the same town.

"Wheresu you gonna live?"

"Well, that's the thing, Dad."

Mas twisted the bottom of his T-shirt.

"We were wondering if we could stay with you for a little while."

Shimmata. The end. The death of a carefree life of going to bed and waking up at any hour he felt compelled to. The death of freely eating ramen and hot dogs (didn't the daughter recently say that the family had adopted some kind of special diet consisting of *wakame,* stringy seaweed, brown rice, and red bean? She claimed it was Japanese but not the Japan Mas knew or liked). The death of leaving his dirty clothes in a trail from the bedroom to the bathroom. The Jensens moving in meant Mas's bad habits had to move out.

"Dad, are you there?"

"Oh, yah. *Orai, yo.*"

Mas cut the conversation short, saying he had to run an errand. Which wasn't entirely untrue but wasn't completely true either.

Before he left the house, he pushed open the door to Mari's old bedroom — still virtually preserved the way she had left it. A twin bed and shag rug with her high school team banners tacked on the wall. Nobody had been allowed to trespass in it; even when Haruo had been staying at Mas's, it was off-limits. And now the ghost would be returning to her old haunts. Would the room be happy? Considering that the thick layer of dust would be cleaned off and perhaps the old shag even ripped up from the hardwood floor, it most likely would be. It probably wouldn't mind being inhabited by three humans of different shapes, colors, and sizes. The question was, how about Mas?

He got into the Ford, and as had become his custom every two weeks, he drove to the Gardeners' Federation co-op. This habit had started on the day of Casey's funeral, in fact. He had stopped by the federation, placed a fertilizer bag over his shoulder as if he were carrying a body sapped of all life or energy, loaded it into the bed of the truck, and driven to the stained-glass church in Koreatown. The rector, dressed in a gown of purple aside from the white tab collar, regretfully told him that the funeral was over. Mas hadn't been interested in attending but had brought gifts instead — a bag of fertilizer for the garden and five thousand dollars, half of Clement and Kiyomi's reward money, to pay for Casey's burial.

He wasn't quite sure why he had made it possible for Casey to have a last resting place. He wasn't sure why he had started to help the community vegetable garden as well. But every two weeks, he'd find something new — organic pesticide, sticks for the carnation stalks — to bring to Koreatown. And normally he did his weekday shopping at the Gardeners' Federation because he didn't want to deal with the brunt of the Eaton Nursery gossip led by Wishbone and Stinky.

As he entered Four Corners and specifically Toy Town this afternoon, a familiar figure came to his aid. Wearing a knit cap even in June, the black man in a T-shirt gestured to an open parking space in front of a store that specialized in soccer balls.

"So how ya doin'?"

Mas handed the homeless man three quarters, two to stick in the meter and one to keep. "My friend gettin' married tomorrow." Mas never shared specifics of his personal life and wondered why a part of him was starting to now.

"That's cool, that's cool. That's fine for other folks to get married. Just make sure it don't catch you. Three times and look where I'm at." The homeless man laughed uproariously, showing off his purplish gums.

The next day at three o'clock in the afternoon Mas made his way to the flower market. In three short hours, the floor of the market had been transformed. Giant silver origami cranes hung from the rafters and every grower had his specialty on display in huge gold-painted plastic vases.

Sweet peas, the color of a pastel rainbow, handpicked by four generations from hunched great-grandmother to toddler. Gardenias and stephanotis from a greenhouse in Carpinteria. Cactus, sunflowers, and baby's breath grown on the hills of Palos Verdes across from a luxury seafront public golf course built by Donald Trump. Exotic orchids, their mouths patterned like snakeskin, from a specialist in Montclair. Brilliant gem-colored roses from Colombia and Ecuador.

Even though the ceremony and reception would be entirely underground, there was plenty of the outdoors filling up the indoors. Mas was admiring some dendrobium from Oxnard when he felt something warm by his elbow.

"Mas, you're going to have to talk to me sometime."

Genessee was dressed in a light blue lace dress that hugged every curve in her body. Mas didn't know that a woman in her sixties could look so juicy. If he had been alone, he would have shoved a fist in his mouth to keep from drooling. Today in his suit, powder blue tie, and hair greased back with Three Flowers oil, he'd just have to swallow.

"You haven't even charged me for my garden. I need to pay you for all those limestone chips and your labor."

Mas had spent seven days and seven nights designing the rock garden for Genessee. He attempted to do all the on-site work while Genessee was away spending time with her grandson. The biggest challenge was finding the anchor for the landscape piece. What could it be? Most Japanese gardens in Los Angeles had their token *tōrō,* stone lantern. Mas needed something different. Natural, he had told Genessee. He started with his own backyard, filled with Chizuko's pots of waxy cymbidium. He searched underneath the overgrown ferns and in the corners crowded with empty plastic planters.

And then he remembered the plant cemetery at Spoon's house. Gaining her and the Buckwheat Beauty's permission this time, he wandered through the beds of sick and dying plants. In the back, underneath, ironically, a wilting bird-of-paradise plant was a large moss-covered stone shaped like the landmark of the nearby city of Eagle Rock. Residents argued whether the rock resembled the head of an eagle or perhaps the outstretched wings of the country's national bird. It didn't matter how the name started or what different people saw in its formation. Those kinds of debates were useless to Mas. There was no changing the shape of the rock. And he would accept his moss-covered find just as it was.

He gathered all the smooth round rocks that Henry the other gardener had given her and relegated them to the outer rim of the garden. The limestone chips filled in the center. But where to place eagle rock? Smack dab in the middle was too obvious, like a dartboard target. No, the rock needed to be placed intuitively in a new home, an egg being laid in a nest. So Mas followed his heart and put the rock in the upper right-hand corner. The rock belonged there, seemed happy there. Out came out the rake, and the limestone chips were combed to simulate ripples around the rock.

"It's beautiful, Mas. I sit out there a couple of times every day. You never know what the light, the shadows bring to the rocks. I never knew rocks could be so beautiful."

Mas grunted. He was proud of what he had done and regretted that he didn't at least have a photo of his finished work.

Genessee sidled up even closer to Mas so that he could smell the tang of her perfume, or perhaps it was just her skin?

"Henry's not my boyfriend, Mas," Genessee whispered in his ear. "Besides, he has a crazy ex-wife. I don't want to be in the middle of that."

She grabbed Mas's hand.

Chu — it happened before Mas could even experience it properly. A peck, or rather half of a full-blown kiss, on the cheek. Mas's face went red and his body tingled all over as if it were in one of those fancy massage chairs. Mas didn't know what to say, so he made an excuse that he had to check in with Haruo.

Haruo found Mas washing his face in the bathroom.

"Taxie lookin' all ova for you. You not sick or nuttin'?" Haruo took hold of Mas's neck to peer into his eyes. Seeing Haruo's fake

302

eye rotate three hundred and sixty degrees wasn't anyone's idea of fun. Mas shuddered and shook his friend loose.

"I'm *orai*."

"Itsu time."

"Oh yah?"

"Yah."

Taxie had already pressed the button for the CD player. A medley of Perry Como songs, Spoon's favorite. He pushed both Mas and Haruo toward the front underneath an iron gazebo decorated with ivy and blue hollyhocks.

In the aisle between two sections of chairs was a butcher paper walkway. At first some of the market guys thought it would be funny to tape together the newspapers featuring a missing Haruo, but luckily Taxie put a stop to it. Down the humble and plain walkway came the Hayakawa girls in birth order. First Debra, then Donna, and finally Dee. They wore simple eggshell-colored shifts and carried bouquets of fresh daisies, Spoon's beloved flower.

As the Buckwheat Beauty made her walk toward the gazebo, she saved a special smile for Mas. She was wearing makeup, but not enough to disguise the freckles.

After Dee came the matron of honor, Sonya de Groot, her beehive hairdo more

303

erect than ever. A yellow silk ribbon had been tied around it and somehow the ridiculous touch suited her. She took her position a couple feet from Mas.

"Funny, I'm a bit nervous," she confessed softly. Lowering her chin, she almost giggled and Mas was afraid that her hair would take a tumble.

Nervous wasn't the emotion that Mas would describe for himself. More like *hazukashii,* embarrassed. All eyes focused on the handful of them. If Haruo had chosen three men to match up with Spoon's girls perhaps Mas would not feel so self-conscious. But he was the main representative, envoy, ambassador for the Mukai side and he felt the full weight of that responsibility.

Of course, he wasn't the only one in the crowd who could vouch for Haruo. Taxie, who was serving as the de facto wedding coordinator, was running around making sure that there were enough chairs for all of the guests. Occasionally a *bang-bang* sounded from him losing a grip on one of the four chairs that he was attempting to carry at one time.

Clement, dressed in a festive Hawaiian shirt, was seated in the front row with an attractive Asian woman with long hair. Next to them were Kiyomi, her husband, and the clan of boys who were poking each other with dead branches they had found on the ground.

On the other side was Geoff de Groot, in a suit that was much too tight for him. He made sure that he sat in the far aisle seat so he could make a quick getaway. Formal occasions weren't the place for flower growers, who much preferred being out in the greenhouse or on the highway making deliveries.

Seated on the Hayakawa side was Itchy, who was tugging at his earlobes as usual. Mas and Itchy had never been close, but the recent revelation of how he forged Ike's and Jorg's death certificates had irretrievably altered their relationship — both for the good and for the bad.

The Eaton Nursery minions were in attendance as well. Stinky was wearing a fat red tie from the seventies while Wishbone had chosen to grow fuzzy sideburns that only burdened his pockmarked face. This wedding would be the talk of Eaton Nursery for at least a couple of days, more if some unexpected disaster befell the nuptials.

Then there was Genessee smiling in her blue dress. He could imagine how the talk would feed off of their "friendship" — not only because they were old, but because Genessee was black Okinawan and a professor to boot. It wouldn't necessarily be a scandal but an unbelievable occurrence, like a child with six fingers on one hand. For some, the unlikely phenomenon was a curse; to others, a sign that miracles do happen.

Mas checked his inside suit pocket and fingered the smooth curve of Spoon's ring. This time the ring would not fall out of his hands. And even if it did, the circle of gold would not land in the belly of a fish but the concrete floor of the flower market, scuffed by decades of flower men and women walking through with their carts and newspaper bouquets and stained by the colors of smashed petals that had fallen loose from the rest of the fold.

Perhaps out of nervousness, Haruo started humming a completely different tune than the Perry Como song. Mas was going to scold him to stop when his eyes locked on a display that had been set up just behind the gazebo. Two *hina* dolls — they must have been Ike's original set because Mas had heard that Spoon had been able to retrieve them from Hina House. The doll man, Klinger, in fact, had not been killed, just banged up enough that both arms were apparently in slings.

The dolls looked, more or less, like the ones that Mas had seen in Spoon's living room. The same delicate white faces and tiny eyes that seemed to move with the light. And then — *ara!* — did Mas imagine it? He could have sworn that underneath the hollyhocks, he had seen the emperor's head bow in recognition of a job well done.

ABOUT THE AUTHOR

Naomi Hirahara is the Edgar Award-winning and Anthony and Macavity Award-nominated author of *Snakeskin Shamisen, Gasa-Gasa Girl,* and *Summer of the Big Bachi,* which was named one of *Chicago Tribune*'s Ten Best Mysteries and Thrillers of 2004 and a *Publishers Weekly* Best Book of the Year. She lives in Southern California.

The employees of Thorndike Press hope you have enjoyed this Large Print book. All our Thorndike, Wheeler, and Kennebec Large Print titles are designed for easy reading, and all our books are made to last. Other Thorndike Press Large Print books are available at your library, through selected bookstores, or directly from us.

For information about titles, please call:
(800) 223-1244

or visit our Web site at:
http://gale.cengage.com/thorndike

To share your comments, please write:
Publisher
Thorndike Press
295 Kennedy Memorial Drive
Waterville, ME 04901